DEAD
MAN
PASS

Also by Peter Dawson
in Thorndike Large Print ®

Renegade Canyon
The Big Outfit
Gunsmoke Graze
Royal Gorge
High Country

This Large Print Book carries the
Seal of Approval of N.A.V.H.

DEAD MAN PASS

Peter Dawson

Thorndike Press • Thorndike, Maine

Copyright © 1954 by The Curtis Publishing Company
Renewed ® 1982 by the Estate of Jonathan Hurff Glidden

All rights reserved.

Published in 1994 by arrangement with Golden West Literary
Agency.

Thorndike Large Print ® Western Series.

The tree indicium is a trademark of Thorndike Press.

The text of this Large Print edition is unabridged.
Other aspects of the book may vary from the original edition.

Set in 16 pt. News Plantin.

Printed in the United States on acid-free, high opacity paper. ∞

Library of Congress Cataloging in Publication Data

Dawson, Peter, 1907–
    Dead man pass / Peter Dawson.
        p.   cm.
    ISBN 1-56054-701-4 (alk. paper : lg. print)
    1. Large type books.   I. Title.
    [PS3507.A848D4   1994]
    813'.54—dc20   94-5474

DEAD

MAN

PASS

Pub (17.95) 6/94

I

This early December blizzard had announced its coming at mid-afternoon yesterday with a howling, blistering-cold gale. The wind had shrieked down across the timbered hills with the booming crash of falling pine and aspen, with steep canyon walls resounding to the low thunder of rock slides as loose, rotten ledges were clawed away. And then, as the inferno seemed to have reached its highest crescendo, purple lightning lanced down out of the frozen, sooty heavens.

That series of thunderclap blasts had finally panicked the eighty mares and geldings. They bolted in terror up into the timber, over the nearby ridges, back along the boulder-strewn bed of the canyon they had been following the past hour.

No sooner had they stampeded than the wind and the lightning died away, a hush settled over the green and tawny land and snow began gently falling. The silence, broken only by distant thunder and the faint whisper of the snow, had let a man unsnarl his nerves and set about putting things right.

By the time Bill Tenn had scoured the slope of the ridge to the east and driven nineteen of his animals back down into the canyon to join the picketed bell mare, the snow was so thick that he had to cast about to find a pocket he remembered lay against the base of a sheer rim in a stand of jackpine close to the west. And as he had been stretching ropes between the scrubby trees, old Early Jordan drove in fourteen more mares and geldings.

Once they finished the makeshift corral they took to the saddle again. In another hour, with the light beginning to fade, the snow had been a smother that at times barely let Tenn see the ears of the sorrel horse he rode. Their count then being sixty-two, he had strapped the bell-mare's bell around the sorrel's neck and announced that he was heading back up the canyon to look for eighteen missing animals.

"In this?" Jordan had argued worriedly. "We'd have to ride a lot of country to find your bones come the thaw next spring."

"It's got to be done, Early."

That had been ten hours and many miles ago. And now as he steadily pushed on down the upper reaches of a wide canyon, Tenn was thinking not so much of the animals he had been unable to find as of his luck in having stumbled upon these eleven lined out across the moonlit expanse of snow ahead.

There had been a few minutes back there just short of midnight when, empty handed and hampered not only by the pitch blackness but by the still heavy fall of snow, he had almost given up. But then, miraculously, the storm had thinned and died away. Stars had presently dusted the inky sky and finally a waning moon had topped the jagged peaks to the east to bathe the timber-shrouded rims in a ghostly cold light. Half an hour later he had heard a neighing in the distance answering the bell. He had found these eleven mares and geldings bunched at the head of a draw in the pines.

For a time his quiet satisfaction over this stroke of luck had warmed him, brought him wide awake and made him forget the bitter cold that cut so deeply into him. But now he was feeling it again, feeling it in spite of the neckerchief tied over his nose and ears and the way he rode with reins wound around the horn, mittened hands stuffed up the sleeves of the stiff canvas wind-breaker. Worst of all, he was dead for sleep. If he didn't soon get to a fire he would be lulled into not caring, which was something he didn't wish to think about.

For some minutes now he had been wondering if this was the right canyon, if in crossing that series of broken ridges some time back he had crossed one too many. He could see no contour, no tree or outcrop he recognized from yesterday, and he told himself, *Ten minutes more and we give this up and start a fire.*

He began counting out the beat of the saddle's rhythmic sway, trying to get it to match the bell's uneven gonging. To warm himself he thought back upon a certain summer when he had camped along a high mountain meadow, and upon a rare leisure hour of fishing a deep clear pool where big rainbow had taken the fly at the tail of a noisy rapids and leaped in flashing abandon.

Suddenly he saw the pinpoint gleam of a fire winking at him from far below.

His wide chest lifted and he tried to shout, afterward laughing at the hoarse croaking of his voice. A strong exultation gripped him and he leaned over and shook the bell until its ear-splitting clanging echoed strongly back from the high rim to the east. He began fumbling under his coat for the horn-handled Colt's, thinking to trigger a shot or two to announce his coming. But then he realized his fingers were too stiff to handle the weapon.

He used the spur now, humming tunelessly, delightedly as he pushed the mares and geldings on at a stiff trot. The gleam of the fire brightened and in another minute he could make out Early Jordan's stooped shape against the light.

Presently, as he walked the sorrel in on the blaze, the old man waded out through the drifts, caught a hold on the bridle and solemnly stated, "Don't you never put me through the likes of this again, son."

"You're a worrier, Early."

Tenn swayed in the saddle, braced himself for the effort and tried to lift a leg over. His boot slipped from the stirrup and he sprawled awkwardly down, Jordan catching him by the arm and keeping him from falling. The crusted snow on his eyebrows, the pinched paleness of his lean face and the bloodshot look of his deep brown eyes roused a sharp concern in the old man. But then when he looked around and smiled sheepishly at his clumsiness, Early Jordan's drooping moustaches straightened in a relieved smile.

"Might've known you'd do it." Jordan's tone was larded with affection, knowing as he did what this must mean to Tenn. The teams off there behind the ropes were the tangible evidence of the man having borrowed to the limit and then of having bargained shrewdly, and now he was almost afraid of the answer he would get as he asked, "How many?"

"Only eleven."

"Only? God A'mighty, what more could you

ask for?" The old man's smile widened then as he reached out and unbuckled Tenn's coat. "Here, peel off and soak up some heat. This is froze stiff as a board."

"Ought to get them behind the ropes first."

"Me, not you." Jordan stripped the canvas from Tenn's broad shoulders and led him in on the fire. He got a tin cup and filled it from a skillet of fresh-boiled coffee simmering on the edge of the coals, saying as he offered it, "Drink this down while I'm gone."

He noticed the way Tenn took the cup in both hands, fondling it with stiff fingers. Now that the light was better he could see what the past twelve hours had taken out of the man, how they had fined down his angular face so that it wore a hawkish look reminding him strongly of old Frank Tenn. And because a lump came to his throat just then he turned away without a further word, taking the sorrel's reins and trudging off into the deep snow.

It took him ten minutes to get the mares and geldings behind the ropes, another five to unsaddle Tenn's horse, picket him and bring him a pan of oats from the pack saddle. When he finally came back to the fire it was to find Tenn hunkered down close to the blaze, blond head bare, spearing thick slices of bacon from a hot skillet with a clasp knife, wolfing them down with pan bread soaked in the sizzling fat.

The old man went on around the fire, pulled his blankets and ground sheet from under the canvas lean-to and dragged them over alongside Tenn, saying as he spread them out, "Fill your belly, sleep the clock around and you'll never know it happened."

Tenn shook his head. "Two, three hours'll do. We'll make it on time if we pull out at first light. On the way back we'll look for —"

"The hell with being on time. Let this man Akers wait a few extra hours for his teams."

"Why? You talk like you and I had never missed a night's sleep before." Tenn's eyes had lost all but a faint trace of their tiredness as he glanced around, his look cheerful, bemused. "Baldy Mountain's off there to the south, Early. Which means we hit the pass road in fifteen, twenty more miles. Once we're over Dead Man we're there."

"Dead Man?"

Tenn nodded. "Dead Man Pass. Years back they strung a road agent from a tree up there and got to calling it that."

"Tell me how to find it and I'll take these jugheads on alone."

"Not a chance. We'll collect the money, get ourselves a shave and a soak in the barber's tub. Then the evening's mine for as much

13

steak and whiskey as you can pack away."

Jordan breathed a slow sigh. "After what we been through maybe I'll take you up on that. I can get awful blind drunk if I put my mind to it." A thought made him frown then, and in another moment he was saying, "You may've once spent half a year in this country. But after ten years what makes you so sure yon can find your pass road with the country buried under all this snow?"

"I was here two months ago. Besides, if you'd driven as many logging hitches as I have down both sides of Dead Man you could find it wearing a blindfold."

Tenn went on eating and Jordan, thinking back across the years, still couldn't quite believe that the gangling youngster he had taught to break his first pony had grown into such a rangy, solid man so like old Frank, the father. Frank had been tall, close to six feet. But this son of his was taller by a good two or three inches. His looks ran more toward Lola's, his mother's, side of the family when you considered the corn-colored hair. But the eyes were like Frank's, dark and hooded by heavy brows. And they had habited themselves to looking squarely at a man, seriously sometimes and sometimes laughing. They were eyes you could trust.

Just now he noticed how the sole of his

friend's left boot was coming loose at the toe, and it gave him the same faintly uncomfortable feeling he had experienced six days ago when Tenn had come to ask him to help in making the long drive down here to the Pinetop country. He had known what a struggle these past five years had been for Tenn, yet they had seen each other so seldom that he hadn't realized how hard the man was pressed, being able to afford nothing better than a near-threadbare outfit. Tenn's canvas coat did little more than cut the wind, his wool shirt was out at the elbows and one knee of his waist-overalls was patched while the other showed signs of wearing through.

But when Jordan thought back on the reason for all this, it seemed right, it couldn't have been otherwise. Lately he'd been able to forget the fall five years ago when the herd of scrawny, fevered Texas longhorns had cut through the east edge of Frank Tenn's range on their way to a reservation agency. He had stopped thinking back on the nightmare of the following month, on what pure hell it had been for him and the crew he bossed for Frank, on how many dozen carcasses they had burned.

That month had nearly ruined a prosperous brand, had put Frank Tenn deep in debt. Then, with Christmas coming on, Frank had died. And Lola had followed him to the grave four months later.

Early Jordan still failed to understand exactly why Bill Tenn had taken on his father's debts. But he had, putting his own name to the notes from the bank, the feed mill and the general store that represented Frank's final struggle for survival. The bank had leased the ranch instead of selling it. Since then Jordan had learned of Tenn chiefly by hearsay, all of which was to his credit. The man hadn't been too proud in the work he chose to bring him the money to meet his notes. One summer he had even hauled buffalo bones and shipped them to a fertilizer firm back in Missouri. Another, a better year, had seen him wearing a badge and keeping a tough town quiet. According to rumor, he could still go back to that town and wear the badge.

Common sense had days ago told Jordan that Tenn was staking a lot on the sale of these teams. And now, thinking of the still missing animals, he abruptly said, "Bill, you're shy six jugheads. Can you turn up with that many short?"

"Akers won't mind."

"But how about you? Does this mean . . ."

Tenn's look turned serious. "We'll swing back through here on our way home and maybe pick up the ones we're shy. But even if we don't I'll clear enough to satisfy the bank."

"Satisfy 'em how?"

"By whittling down what I owe so they'll wind up the lease come next spring and let me move back home and start running the brand again."

Early Jordan's deep-lined face went slack with wonder. "You're that close to being out from under?"

"That close, Early."

"I'm damned," the old man stated solemnly. "You've made it add up mighty quick."

"I've had luck."

"It's been more than luck, son."

Tenn gave Jordan a thoughtful stare. "Which reminds me. I've been meaning to ask if you'd consider moving out home to boss a two man crew in the beginning."

"Would I!" Early Jordan's eyes brightened with a look of sheer delight. "Why, I . . . I been dreaming of the day you and me could . . ."

His voice momentarily gave out on him and, dropping his head and blinking the moistness from his eyes, he said quietly, "You've just hired yourself a hand."

Pinetop's main street, Alder, ran out the head of the valley at right angles to the foot of the pass road. A quarter of a mile beyond the last house, and in a thin stand of pine footing the steep face of the mountain, sprawled a disorderly array of slab shacks and tents sagging under the weight of new snow. Littered among them were stacks of timbers and barrels, ranks of wagons and two-wheeled dump carts. And finally there was a big corral with a blacksmith's shanty alongside it.

The reason for this work camp was a gaping twenty-foot-square hole in the face of the mountain, beyond which each day the straight line of a new grade crept eastward foot by foot. Work crews this frosty, sunny morning moved raggedly along the packed snow of the grade, for the most part made up of eight-man teams of Chinese pulling carts filled with granite rubble mucked from the tunnel.

Now, at a few minutes past ten o'clock, Samuel Akers stood at a window of the one near-permanent log building in the camp, his office. He was so tall, topping six feet by a good five inches, that his massive frame was stooped slightly to let him peer through the glass. The features of his face were as heavy, as thick as the rest of him, yet they somehow contrived to give him a look of rugged handsomeness in a boldly positive way that invariably attracted a woman's attention and also made most men take a liking to him.

His face was set thoughtfully now as he looked beyond the nearby corral to watch the activity along the grade. It wasn't often that the man's driving energy permitted him to idle. Yet it had a few minutes ago struck him that today, December the tenth, might be his birthday. The thought had put him in a rare reflective mood.

He wasn't certain of the exact day on which he'd been born though he was sure it had been during the second week in December thirty years ago in 1854. He had never known a father and his faint recollection of his mother was made unwelcome by the realization that the only home she had ever given him was a drab room over a riverfront saloon in Hannibal, Missouri.

The birthdays, or birth weeks, he could recall were few. One, long ago, had seen him jumping from the boiler deck of a river boat somewhere along the lower Mississippi after stealing a stranger's poke. Another, more recent, had found him in the camp of some renegade Cheyennes haggling over what he should be paid for ten barrels of whiskey he had stolen. And still another, his twenty-fourth, had let him lay the foundations for his present affluence when, in a day and night session in a New Orleans gambling house, he had won upward of eight thousand dollars chiefly because he could read the marked cards the house had bought from a friend of his the previous month.

A hard life, an utter lack of scruples and an innate shrewdness had brought Sam Akers a long way from his obscure beginnings. His affability, his physical bigness that let him fear no one, made him an easy man to get on with. Life on the river boats and a long acquaintance with the pleasure parlors of St. Louis and New Orleans had taught him rudimentary manners and given him a taste for clothes. Finally, his out-giving nature and his habit of spending money freely invariably made him friends.

These qualities had profited him three years ago when, on buying a dying dray business from an impoverished widow, he had secured a contract to repair bridges and grade along a washed out spur of the Cheyenne and Western Railroad. Because he had finished that contract with despatch, he had secured others.

The digging of this tunnel for the C. & W. was Sam Akers' biggest venture into legitimate business so far. It involved working upward of a hundred men in speculating on his ability to haul rock from the mountain at a cost well under the cubic yardage payment the railroad made him. So far he was realizing a tidy profit.

Just now as he squinted against the harsh snow glare he all at once noticed something that caught his hard attention. A herd of horses had stopped traffic along the grade and was spilling over it, lining out in this direction toward the corral. For a long moment Akers studied the two riders driving the animals. Then a broad smile eased the seriousness from his blocky face.

He glanced around at a slight, balding man working at a desk in the room's back corner. "Fred, believe it or not, here come our teams. What was that saddle tramp's name?"

"Tramp? You mean Tenn? William Tenn, I think it was." Pushing back his green eyeshade and laying his pen between the pages of a ledger, the bookkeeper rose and came to the window, shortly remarking, "Fine looking animals. Come to think of it, Tenn was due today."

Sam Akers nodded absent-mindedly, his thoughts already running on ahead to tomorrow and the next day as he calculated how much these teams would speed the work. But then in his devious way he was thinking of something else, and the pleasantness left his eyes to be replaced by a speculative scowl. And abruptly he was asking, "Where's Buck?"

"You sent him out to move that powder wagon away from the big tent."

Akers turned, quickly crossing to the window at the opposite side of the room. Lifting its lower sash wide, he leaned on the sill and bawled loudly, "Buck, want to see you," closing the window on hearing a faint shout answering him.

Standing alongside Fred Stone again and watching Tenn's teams beginning to file in through the corral gate, he was thinking, *It's worth a try.* And as he saw Tenn shortly rein his claybank horse this way from the corral gate, he sourly commented, "I've seen better horseflesh in my time."

Fred Stone looked up at him in faint puzzlement. But then, warned by Akers' mood, the bookkeeper turned back to the desk in silence. And by the time Tenn's boots sounded across the stoop beyond the door Stone was once again penning his precise figures in the ledger.

Bill Tenn entered the office to find them that way, the bookkeeper engrossed in his work, big Sam Akers at the window frowning in the direction of the corral. Neither man glanced his way as he came in on the counter closing off the front third of the room, so that the cheerful look on his unshaven face thinned a little as he asked, "Well, Akers, how do they look?"

Akers turned, measuring Tenn aloofly a moment before asking, "How many?"

"Seventy-three." Puzzled by the other's

manner, Tenn went on, "That storm yesterday —"

"How long since they've had a feed?
They're damned bony."

Tenn thought, *What is this?* bridling, "Now
wait a minute. They're in fine shape. Night
before last we had them on that grass along
Pot Creek. Early and I —"

Checking his words at the sound of the door
opening, he turned to see a medium tall and
solidly built man come into the room. A moment later Akers was saying, "Buck, our teams
are here. Better get out there and look 'em
over. Tenn, this is Flynn, my foreman."

Flynn and Tenn shook hands, Flynn smiling
good-naturedly to say, "Now we can get that
hole dug in a hurry."

Tenn liked the man, liked the firmness of
his grip and a certain shyness in his glance,
though he was only remotely aware of this
in his preoccupation of trying to understand
Akers' ill humor. And now the big man, looking out the window again, abruptly remarked,
"There's the ugliest bay ever foaled. That
bull-nosed gelding with the white stockings."

There was no need for Tenn to go to the
window to answer, "He'll outpull 'most any
other in the bunch. Cost me forty dollars, so
I don't make much on him."

"Much?" Akers echoed, his glance whipping around. "You don't make anything. You lose five."

Both Flynn and Stone were looking at Tenn now, seeing his lean face go loose in surprise and puzzlement. There was an awkward, dead silence in which the whisper of burning wood in the corner stove was plainly audible. Then Tenn was asking, "How does that figure?"

"Simple arithmetic. You're collecting thirty-five a head."

Bill Tenn felt the blood rush to his face, felt the beginning of panic blending with the hard anger rising in him. Yet he managed to keep his tone even as he drawled, "Say that again. Say it right. Forty-five dollars a head."

Akers stiffened, turning, and laying both hands on the counter as his beetling glance bored in on Tenn. "Just what the hell are you talking about?"

"About looking up the Denver market in a paper right here two months ago. About settling on a price two dollars below the market. About your ordering forty teams at forty-five dollars the animal."

The big man's jaw muscles corded in anger. Wheeling around, he asked sharply, "Fred, what was the price we agreed on?"

Hesitating a moment, Fred Stone blandly answered, "You know how deaf I am when I work."

Akers' look turned ugly at this insubordination, though that quality had faded from his glance when he turned to stare beyond Tenn and ask, "Buck, what price did I tell you we'd settled on?"

"Don't think you ever mentioned one to me, Sam."

Now the big man eyed Tenn in open belligerence, bursting out, "By God, you don't get away with this. You don't have me over any barrel. I'll haul rock all winter with those Chinks harnessed to my wagons before I let you steal me blind."

Those uncompromising words stung Bill Tenn like the lash of a whip. The utter incongruity of what he was hearing appalled him. He lifted a hand and rubbed it across his eyes, trying to grasp the fact that this was the Sam Akers who had sixty days ago been so easy-going and patently honest.

He saw weeks of work gone for nothing, saw himself set back a year, two perhaps, in having to sell his teams on the low winter market. This was something he could scarcely yet believe, and now as rage and indignation finally had their way with him he asked tonelessly, "You mean to stand there and tell me I ever agreed to deliver harness broke mares and geldings at thirty-five dollars a head?"

"You've got ears. That's what I said."

Tenn slowly shook his head. "It's no dice, Akers."

"Then get those nags the hell out of my corral."

Bill Tenn's eyes blazed in a brief, stunned outrage. Then he was drawling with deceptive mildness, "If I ride out of here you don't see me again. No man can give me his word and go back —"

"Grab him, Buck! Toss him out!"

Tenn started swinging around. He was a fraction of a second too late, for as he moved Flynn's arms locked tightly about him, pinning his elbows to his waist so hard that the Colt's at his belt ground painfully against hip-bone.

Rage made him ignore the pain and lifted him out of his tiredness then, roused the raw-hide toughness in him. Planting his boots wide and throwing himself sharply forward against Flynn's weight, he wheeled in a convulsive heave that lifted the foreman's boots from the floor, broke his hold and threw him viciously against the counter's corner. Flynn lost his balance and fell heavily into the wall, his shoulder colliding with Akers and jarring the big man back a step.

Tenn was breathing heavily as he faced them, his canvas coat torn open and one buckle dangling from its fastener. And Sam Akers,

26

glimpsing the horn-handled Colt's sagging from a shell belt high along Tenn's thigh, and also noticing the wild, killing light shining in the man's eyes, stayed the quick reach of his right hand below the counter's edge, instead lifting the hand and laying it carefully on the wood.

Bill Tenn caught that gesture and his eyes went agate hard. "Go ahead, reach for it." His tone was larded with a scalding contempt and hostility, and now his glance shifted to Flynn, then back to Akers once more. "You're a sorry pair. Akers, I once jailed a rustler a lot like you. Only he was a better man. Because it was known he'd never gone back on his word."

"Haul your freight out of here," Akers told him.

Tenn smiled sparely, coldly. "So you played me for a sucker. Figured to reach right into my pocket and help yourself to seven hundred and thirty dollars. And here I took your word as being gilt edged."

He waited for Akers to speak and, getting no response, drawled, "I'll take my licking and like it. Like it because I'll know you're sweating without teams. Dig your damned tunnel by hand." Deliberately, he added, "Akers, you're crooked as a green rope. Feel like arguing the point?"

"Go on, get out."

"I will. The air's mighty foul in here."

Tenn backed to the door and opened it, his glance not straying from the pair. As he stepped out of sight, slamming the door hard, Akers said sharply, "Let him go," to stop Flynn's lunge toward the door.

The big man moved over to peer out of the window, seeing Tenn riding away toward the corral gate where his helper waited. He looked around at his foreman then. "First time I ever saw a man handle you that easy, Buck."

"Handle me?" Flynn echoed, his look outraged. "Why, he . . . it couldn't happen again, not ever."

Akers ignored him, glancing at Stone. "You were sure a big help."

Stone gave a slow shake of the head. "That was a mistake, Sam. He won't be back, not that one."

"Want to lay money on it? Look at him. So hard up his toes are damn' near through the ends of his boots. He'll be back and he'll sell for thirty-five a head."

"Suppose you're wrong?"

Akers lifted his heavy-muscled shoulders. "Then we keep on like we are till spring, until we can buy teams. I tried to buy, the deal fell through. What can Ralph Burgess say to that? Nothing. The job takes longer and I maybe collect more money than if I'd hurried the digging."

Fred Stone's look was tinged with faint disgust. "If I were you I'd admit my mistake and pay Tenn what you agreed to."

"If you were me you wouldn't be sitting there drawing twenty dollars a week, Fred."

Buck Flynn was momentarily puzzled by this interchange, though when he fully grasped its meaning he checked the impulse to protest, thinking in an awed way that perhaps something had escaped him, that what he had just witnessed must be still another example of Sam Akers' uncanny acumen in business dealings. Besides, there was something in his relations with this shrewd and unpredictable giant that didn't give him the right to be too critical. That was a thing he wasn't quite sure of yet.

So, shrugging mentally, he left the office and went back to work.

Over the next hour Bill Tenn was harder put to calm Early Jordan than he was to control his own resentment over the outcome of his meeting with Akers. The old man at first raged, insisting that the two of them should go back and force a showdown with Akers. But then as they drove the teams on away from the camp Jordan began listening to reason, to Tenn's argument that the first thing to do was see a lawyer.

They found a steep-walled pocket against the hills close above the head of the street and drove the mares and geldings into it, then began cutting brush to close its narrow mouth. But after ten minutes of this Jordan's impatience got the better of him. "Leave this to me and get on into town. Find a way of making that big moose ante what he owes."

Riding on down Pinetop's main street some minutes later, Tenn had passed the intersection at the center of town before finding what he was looking for, a board sign hanging over a first-floor doorway proclaiming, *John H. Updyke, Att'y, Notary, Deeds, Wills.*

He tied the claybank at the pole in front of the building, and some five minutes after he had entered the office John Updyke's bony frame was slouched in the tilted swivel-chair behind his flat-topped desk, one knee braced against the desk's edge as he listened. The lawyer was sucking a cold briar pipe and, typically, paid not so much attention to what he was hearing as to the manner of the man who was talking.

There was a quiet dignity and purposefulness about this tall, unshaven stranger that made you forget his near-shabby outfit, Updyke was thinking. Tenn had a habit of making words count, of unconsciously flattering his listener's intelligence by not dwelling on the obvious, as now when he said, "Makes me feel like a ten year old kid, not having put the whole thing down in writing."

"Not necessarily," Updyke was quick to say. "Nine tenths of the business around here, mine included, is done by one man taking another at his word."

"What've I run into? Doesn't the town know this bird's slippery?"

"Can't answer that, Tenn. Akers is too new here to prove much of anything. He's a free spender and has a lot of friends." The lawyer laughed softly, shedding his soberness in a way that made Tenn aware of his being younger than he had supposed, probably in his middle thirties. "There's the rub, as Will Shakespeare would say. Bring this to court and you'd have a hard time finding twelve men who didn't know Akers and like him."

"Then I'll take my licking and clear out." Tenn reached to pants pocket. "How much do I owe you for your trouble?"

"Not a cent. I haven't done anything for you."

Tenn shook his head, laying a silver dollar on the desk. "Rather not stretch my credit."

Updyke shrugged, rising now as Tenn started for the door. But then the lawyer was they climbed the steps to the *Buena Vista*'s closed-in veranda Tenn's feeling of gratefulness prompted him to say, "It's mighty good of you to be doing this."

"Maybe I'm playing for that tenth chance along with you," Updyke soberly stated. "Akers happens to be trying to charm one of the most delightful girls I know, Buck Flynn's sister. I'm privately of the opinion that she's far too good for him."

"Then here's hoping we have luck."

But in five more minutes Bill Tenn knew he wasn't going to have any luck. They had found Burgess in a front upstairs parlor, found him alone studying a survey chart spread out across a big oak table. He was a short, rotund man of middle age and he wasn't particularly friendly as John Updyke made the introduction. And when Tenn had briefly answered his brusque question as to what they wanted, he gave an emphatic shake of the head.

"There's not a prayer of my helping. Not even if I took your word for this against Sam's. We don't have any hold on him beyond seeing he makes good on his contract. How he does it is his lookout."

When Tenn only arched his brows, shrugged and said nothing, Burgess eyed the lawyer with a wry smile. "You wouldn't believe what double-barreled hell we catch from

He paused, noticing the way Tenn's glance had suddenly sharpened. "Something on your mind?"

"Maybe there is," Bill Tenn softly answered.

Burgess gave Updyke a puzzled look, then eyed Tenn again. "What?"

"Something you just said. About how fine it'd be to have engines working this end of your tunnel."

"It'd be better than fine. It'd be a miracle."

"Then why don't you put them to work across here?"

"Why?" Burgess echoed in strong annoyance. "Because there's no possible way of getting them here."

"No? Why not haul them up and over Dead Man?"

Ralph Burgess was momentarily held speechless by surprise. But then he laughed, though with no amusement whatsoever. "You're wasting my time, Tenn. I've got a lot to do. Now if you'll —"

"Are these engines you're talking about the ones we see running through Red Rock?" Tenn cut in.

"The same."

"Then why not haul them over here?"

John Updyke saw Burgess's face redden in anger and hastily put in, "Easy, Ralph. Let's listen to what he has to say."

"Why should I?" the engineer asked tartly. "It's a hairbrained notion." Looking at Tenn, he asked, "Would you know what a Mogul weighs?"

"No. But I know how three fifty foot pine logs each four feet through at the butt end handle on a set of logging sleds. If that load wouldn't weigh more than one of your engines, I'll split all three logs into matchwood for you."

A look of incredulity, of near-eagerness momentarily rid Burgess's glance of its bridling quality. But then he was lifting a hand in a deprecatory gesture. "You don't know what you're saying, man. One of those engines will go sixteen, eighteen tons. Haul that much weight up a crooked road without dropping it over a —"

"Burgess, that road was built mainly for logging." Tenn interrupted with a look of apology. "It was graded and the bends widened twelve years ago when old Pace bought that timber tract up Baldy Mountain. I know because I've hauled more logs down both sides than you could stack along the main street here. Heavier loads than one of your Moguls, too."

The engineer gave John Updyke a baffled, uncertain glance that made the lawyer quietly insert a word. "Sounds like an idea worth considering, Ralph."

Suddenly Burgess burst out, "Damn it, I want straight talk. This is important enough to —"

"You're getting straight talk."

"You hauled your logs down, not up."

"Hauling up is easiest. It takes more teams, sure. But you're forgetting I own thirty-six teams."

"I'm not forgetting that you're looking for a way of selling them, too." Burgess's look still bridled, though he added, "Go on, let's hear more."

"What more do you want to know? That on a pull with a heavy load you can use block and tackle to help your teams? Or that on a downgrade with a heavy sled you wrap your runner logs with chain and drag shelf rock to put the right brake on your load?"

Ralph Burgess swore softly, now openly impressed with what he was hearing. And for the first time his tone was almost mild as he said, "Tenn, I shoot straight with a man. I expect the same of him. If what you're saying is true, if you can haul Moguls across here for me, I'll keep you busy for a year. You can haul cars, rail, ties. You can . . ."

As he hesitated, Tenn quietly inserted, "Say the word and I'll get at it."

"Sam Akers wouldn't like it one damn' bit if you bring this off, my friend. We've got a right to do it, but it'd cost him a pretty penny."

"Good. If that's the case I'll work for nothing to see it happen."

"He might make it hard for you."

"Suppose you let me worry about friend Akers."

That mildly-worded statement carried considerable weight with Burgess, who was all at once struck by the thought, *This bird could maybe be just as tough as he is easy to get on with.* And now a real excitement began lifting in him, though he tried not to show it as he casually queried, "What would your price be for hauling two Moguls over the pass?"

Tenn appeared momentarily uncertain of himself. Finally a rueful smile touched his flat-planed face. "I wouldn't begin to know how to name you a price."

The engineer reached for a pad of paper and a pencil on the table, offering them. "Sit down and whittle out a figure."

Bill Tenn could scarcely believe what was happening to him, and in his bewilderment he felt suddenly out of his depth in this exchange. Burgess noticed that and gave Updyke an eloquent glance, for he was thinking that nine out of ten men would right now be bluffing, deciding to take advantage of him in the knowledge that he would probably pay out of all reason to see his Moguls working the Pinetop grade. Yet Tenn wasn't of that breed, and in real gratefulness the engineer laid the pad on the table, saying,

"All right, I'll lend you a hand. First thing we do is set a weekly charge for your teams." He paused, an unexpected smile breaking across his round face as he eyed Updyke. "Y'know, John, if we can pull this off I'll have rail laid as far as Goose Lake by the time this tunnel's open."

"Thank Tenn, not me, Ralph."

Bill Tenn had scarcely been listening, and now as the lawyer finished he put in a quiet word. "I've got one man with me I'd like to see taken care of. An old timer who used to rod a big crew for my father. I'm paying him ten dollars a week, and so far as I know he doesn't have work for the rest of the winter. Could we keep him on as long as I work for you?"

"You work for yourself, not me," Burgess corrected him. "You'll be a contractor, the same as Sam Akers is. It sounds like your friend could straw-boss the job. So we'll put him down as getting twenty a week."

The engineer had to drop his glance in embarrassment at the look of gratefulness Tenn gave him. "Let's say fifteen a week is a fair fee for each of your teams providing I furnish feed," he went on gruffly. "We've got chain, block and tackle, 'most everything you'll need in the Granite warehouse. Say you need six good men —"

"Better make it eight. We'll need teamsters most of all. And if we can find a few who know axe work it'd make it that much simpler."

"I'll find you teamsters, loggers, anything you need." The engineer's manner was betraying a real excitement now as, eyeing Updyke, he breathed, "Damned if I don't buy you a fifty cent cigar for bringing Tenn around to see me, John."

An hour later Bill Tenn left the hotel in the biting cold of as fine and sunny an afternoon as he could remember. In his pocket he carried a signed contract involving a weekly profit to him of almost exactly what he would have made on the sale of his teams to Sam Akers. And there was the promise of many weeks of work ahead.

That evening at dusk Ralph Burgess and Sam Akers waited on the *Buena Vista*'s glassed-in veranda for the Granite stage, due in ten minutes. It was Burgess who interrupted their idle talk by nodding out onto the street, saying, "Here comes your friend."

Akers took in the two riders swinging through a shallow drift toward a tie-rail below, recognizing Tenn's high shape astride a leggy sorrel. He put down the impulse to say something belittling, instead telling the engineer, "Wish he hadn't taken it the way he did, Ralph. It was a plain and simple misunderstanding."

"You may wish later on you'd paid his price."

Akers was watching Tenn and Early Jordan cross the walk toward the hotel's saloon entrance, noticing that Tenn had had a shave and was wearing a new pair of waist-overalls. He was inwardly galled at realizing that this was the man responsible for Burgess's idea of hauling engines over the pass. With the engines at work he would automatically be paid a lower rate for his share in digging the tunnel, and there was unmistakable venom underlying his words now as he stated, "Don't trust that joker too far, Ralph."

Burgess made no comment, a fact that only increased the big man's feeling of resentment over what had happened today. He somehow managed to hide his disappointment and anger until the engineer had climbed into the stage, until the coach finally pulled away into the gathering darkness. But then as he turned up the street he finally let go the hold on his emotions and began swearing, muttering in impotent rage as he crossed the intersection.

Such was Sam Akers' frame of mind tonight that for the half hour he paced the shovelled paths far out toward the head of Alder Street. Only at the end of that interval had his rage over the news Ralph Burgess had given him worn itself out to leave him comparatively calm, able to think ahead once more.

How to meet this threat of Tenn hauling engines over the pass was the immediate problem. He thought of a number of ways of dealing with Tenn, none of which were quite to his liking. Presently, feeling the need of sharing his worry with someone, he decided to have a talk with Buck Flynn and turned back down to the center of town, walked past the stores and then along the paths fronting the down-street houses.

Over the past four months since coming to Pinetop, Sam Akers had followed this same course many, many times. And as he shortly approached the gate of a yard fronting a two-story house closely flanked by its neighbors, he was remembering his first visit here on a late summer evening, and his first glimpse of Sheila, Buck Flynn's sister.

That had been a memorable evening for Akers in one respect, undermining as it had a well-established conceit that had made him believe wedlock to be a life for fools or the faint-hearted. In the weeks since, visiting the house first on the pretext of having business with Buck, then more boldly in an open courting of the chestnut-haired Sheila, Akers' views on marriage had shifted from one pole to its opposite. In a way that was typical of him, he had come to accept as a certainty the fact that Sheila Flynn would one day be his wife.

Walking the cleared path leading to the house now, he felt the same strong annoyance as always at seeing the sign hanging from the porch railing, *Board, Dollar a Day*. For in his thoughts of the future, in picturing his life with Sheila in a city far from here, he had no intention of ever letting it be known that his wife had once run a boarding house, though it had never once occurred to him that this was a disproportionate stand to take considering his own background.

This unwelcome and recurring thought was rudely interrupted just now as, coming in on the porch steps, he heard the door above him slam. Glancing up, he saw Buck Flynn's stocky shape outlined against the door's frosted glass. And he said loudly, with a forced cheerfulness, "Was just on the way in to see you, Buck."

Flynn swung sharply around in startlement,

then came to the porch's edge. "And I was damn' well just on my way find you."

The man's belligerent tone jolted Akers. Not beginning to understand it, he nevertheless mildly told his foreman, "Something's happened I don't like one bit. Come along out here while I tell you about it."

"You're right," came Flynn's clipped rejoinder. "Something has happened. Only not what you're thinking."

He came down the steps now and Akers led the way back to the street path, sensing trouble and thankful they weren't to be inside where Sheila could hear the argument he knew must be coming.

He was turning out the gate when Flynn suddenly burst out. "What a hairbrain thing to do, sending that crew up into the hole this afternoon to muck out more ore. Didn't we agree we were too close under the road, that we'd lay off until we could put in shoring?"

Here was the one man around Pinetop, anywhere in fact, who could use such a tone on Akers. The big man's tolerance of this Irishman's sometimes blunt way of talking to him was tempered by only one thing, the fact that Buck was Sheila's brother. So he stifled the hard anger that rose in him now and, stopping, turned to say, evenly, "They didn't dig higher. They worked a side pocket."

"That drain tunnel's finished, you fool. And this camp's full of hard rock men who know the looks of silver highgrade. Let one of them —"

"But that was just a bunch of Chinks this afternoon." Stung by Flynn calling him a fool, Akers nevertheless kept his mounting anger in check. "I had them haul the paydirt to the outlet and then cover it with ordinary stuff, just like we did the main batch. If they noticed anything, they think we're still cutting that air shaft."

"What are you, all hog?" Flynn was suddenly raging, shouting as he glared up at Akers. "How much do you want? Who found that porphyry and knew it was silver? Me. And who got the idea of following the vein up and calling it an air shaft? Only I made my mistake in the beginning, made it by letting you in on it. If you're so confounded greedy, why don't you do as I wanted to at the start, you and me file on that ground so we can haul our ore straight across to Granite?"

Those scalding words roused a cold fury in Akers. "You bull-headed Mick," he said tonelessly, quietly. "Don't you rough me with your tongue."

He reached out all at once trying to get a grip on Flynn's coat front. Fast as he was, the Irishman was faster, lunging back out of his reach. Then, unbelievably, Flynn clawed his coat aside, jerked a gun from his belt and levelled it.

For an instant before his foreman spoke again, Sam Akers was suddenly realizing what this meant, that somehow he had to get the upper hand here. But then Flynn was hefting the Colt's, saying, "This is just in case you try and break me in two. Now you're going to stand there and take what I have to say. To begin with . . ."

He abruptly checked himself as the sharp, staccato sound of a woman's steps striking the brick path opposite shuttled across to him. In another moment he went on in a quieter tone, "To begin with, I'm quitting you as of now."

"You saved me having to say it."

Akers' statement crowded Buck Flynn beyond the point of reason once more. "What was it Tenn called you this morning? 'Crooked as a new rope.' You damn' well are. What you pulled on him finally tipped me off on what a sidewinder I've been tied up with. But I'm through. I don't wait for you to finish that confounded tunnel before I mine that ore. Because tomorrow I go across to Granite and file a claim —"

"Do that and every man working the tunnel

46

will quit his job, go up the mountain and start digging."

"Who the hell cares? Should I cry if you go broke on this job? Only don't worry, I'm filing the claim in both our names."

"Better think it over, Buck."

Akers had spoken only to be saying something, to stall for time. For abruptly he knew that this man had it in his power to all but ruin him. It was bad enough to be losing him as foreman, for good men like Flynn were hard to find. But worse than that was the real possibility that the Irishman would lose him his work gang.

Buck Flynn chose this moment to say the thing that ended any chance of their ever healing their differences, a thing that drove Sam Akers to the fierce urge to kill. "Get this, Sam. From now on you keep clear of Sheila. Because I'm telling her a few things about you."

He waited for Akers to speak. Then, as the silence ran on, he voiced a final, deadly serious word. "Just in case you think my knees are knockin', I'm on my way to the hotel for a drink. If you've got a mind to argue this further, you'll find me there. With this."

The faint lamplight shining from the parlor window of the Flynn house let Sam Akers see the spare way the Irishman hefted his Colt's before he turned and walked away into the heavy shadows up the path.

Flynn kept the gun in his hand, looking behind him until the big man's massive shape was lost to sight in the blackness.

This had been the evening Bill Tenn had promised Early Jordan last night, an evening of celebration. And now as the old man's head began to nod, when his sleep and drink-heavy eyes finally closed and stayed that way, Tenn nudged him, drawling, "Time to ride and hit the blankets, Early."

He got up from the table beyond the *Buena Vista*'s long bar and hauled his friend to his feet. Jordan grinned sheepishly, muttering, "First time four glasses ever . . . ever got to me this . . ."

Taking his arm, Tenn told him, "There'll be other times. More good nights here and in Granite. Let's travel."

He steadied the old man on their way past a faro and a poker layout, then as far as the door. He pushed the batwing panels wide and, holding Jordan's arm, started out onto the walk. That moment Buck Flynn's wide and stocky shape moved in out of the shadows.

Flynn saw Jordan first, quickly read his condition and shoved him aside. Then he saw a second man in his way, though with Tenn's back to the light he didn't recognize him. Still angry from his talk with Akers, in no mood to give way to anyone, he reached out and with a sweep of his arm tried to move Tenn aside.

Bill Tenn knew who this was, and as Flynn's hand slammed him against the door's frame he braced himself, blocking the way. "Not so fast there."

He wasn't forgetting what the Irishman had tried to do to him this morning and he moved forward now, his shoulder ramming Flynn. Sudden recognition showed in the other's eyes as he was jolted back a stride. And as Tenn came onto the walk he knew he had started something.

If he had any doubt as to exactly what was to happen, Flynn gave him only a second to rid himself of it. Saying softly, "No you don't, bucko," Flynn drew back his right arm and swung viciously, fast.

Tenn saw the blow coming, rolled out of the way and threw all the weight of his wide shoulder behind a punch that drove deep into the other's midsection. He knew that this would have to be fast, knew that between two glasses of whiskey and his tiredness he was no match for the tough, heavy-muscled Irishman. So now as Flynn was jarred back and his arms dropped, Tenn swung hard at the man's face and connected, swung again with a power that rocked Flynn's head sharply back.

Quite suddenly the Irishman's wide bulk went limp, dropped. With some amazement Tenn realized that the fight was over, that his last blow had caught the other on the point of the chin and slammed his head hard back against the hotel wall. And as he looked down to see Buck Flynn sitting against the wall staring dazedly at the snowy walk, he was aware of several men standing nearby in the light of the window.

"Lord, Buck can do better than that," someone stated in an awed way.

Tenn turned to find Early Jordan leaning against a nearby awning post, chin on chest, dozing. He laughed softly, exultantly, feeling strangely cleansed inside as he put an arm about the old man's shoulders and steered him down the walk. A crowd was gathering in front of the saloon when he and Jordan shortly rode past and up the street.

The fire at their camp was burned down to a bed of dying coals. After Tenn had heaped branches on it he found the old man rolled in the blankets, quietly snoring. In five more minutes he had unsaddled both animals, turned them in behind the brush barrier and was himself crawling between the blankets.

For a time he lay thinking back on all that

had happened today, thinking of Sam Akers and Buck Flynn, of John Updyke and finally of Burgess. Tomorrow he would have to go to Updyke, thank him again and . . .

Later, much later, he felt his shoulder being roughly shaken. He opened his eyes to see a shape bending over him, to see the fire's feeble light reflected dully from a revolver's barrel.

He pushed up onto an elbow, and the man above stepped back out of reach, motioning sparely with his weapon. "On your feet."

Tenn was wide awake now, noticing two more men on the far side of the fire, both carrying rifles. He quickly glanced up at the nearest man. "What's wrong?"

The other smiled mirthlessly, half turning to call to his companions, "What's wrong, he wants to know."

Staring down with an ugly look then, he said, "We've found Buck Flynn, is what's wrong. Found him where you left him there along the street with the back of his head caved in."

II

Pinetop's snowy, rutted streets were alive with traffic on this third sunny afternoon following Bill Tenn's arrest for the murder of Buck Flynn. The tie rails at the center of town were crowded with saddle animals, sleds, wagons and lighter rigs, and the day had so far seen two runaways.

The hard board benches filling the meeting hall above Saunders' hardware store were packed. This was the second and final day of the trial, and those who couldn't force their way up the stairs and into the big room loafed on the walk below, with only a few men betting on what the verdict would be. The three saloons were doing a thriving business, the play at their gaming tables as heavy as on a Saturday night.

Judge Haldeman began giving his instructions to the jury shortly after two o'clock. And as Bill Tenn heard his name repeatedly and sometimes acidly mentioned, he could feel his face growing hot and his hands moist. It didn't ease the tightness of his nerves to have John Updyke, his lawyer, once lean close to him and whisper,

"Try not to listen, Bill. All this doesn't mean as much as you think."

After that Bill really tried not to listen. The hearings today and yesterday had roused such disbelief and fury in him that he was now unable to comprehend quite how all this had happened. John Updyke had defended him doggedly, even brilliantly at times. Yet public indignation was calling for a victim and the prosecution had made a strong case of one that, in the beginning, had been weak.

Just now he glanced nervously back across the packed room, hard aware of the crowd's animosity. But the thing that made the deepest impression on him was the change he saw in Sheila Flynn, who sat at the far end of the front row next to her mother.

Yesterday morning, as the jury was being picked and sworn in, his attention had been taken by a tall and slender girl with chestnut hair making her way along the crowded side aisle to the one vacant place on the front bench behind the makeshift railing that separated the court from the spectators. The girl was striking looking, yet it was her complete lack of self-conscionsness as the crowd stared at her — that and the warm responsiveness of her smile as she once spoke to a friend — that most impressed him in the beginning.

Later, finding this girl the one refreshing element in his otherwise hostile surroundings, he had been unable to keep from glancing at her now and then. And as he studied her he discovered flaws in her features that saved her from being merely pretty, that instead gave her face real character and an indefinable inner beauty.

For one thing, her nose was straight, even subtly aquiline, lacking the coquettish uptilt fashionably considered to be the mark of a woman's liveliness of spirit. Yet this girl did have spirit he saw presently, that quality becoming evident in the animation her green eyes betrayed once as she turned to talk to a woman seated behind her. Her nose and cheeks were lightly dusted with freckles, despite which her face wore a subtle clear loveliness set off by hair that glinted with coppery highlights as the sun from a window beyond her touched it.

It had been perhaps an hour after he first noticed her that she looked his way unexpectedly to find his glance full upon her. The next instant he had been shocked by the loathing, the resentment, that shone in her eyes. Not long afterward he had asked John Updyke who she might be and had only then realized how much reason she had to hate even the sight of him.

These two days had worked a visible change in Sheila Flynn. She still stood out sharply from the other women in the crowd. But now she was showing the strain of these torturing hours of listening to the details of the killing. Her eyes wore a lackluster, tired look, her face had lost its glow of health and was pale.

It so happened that at this moment she seemed to feel the weight of his stare, for her head came around and their eyes met. Yet this time, in contrast to yesterday, all that showed in her glance was a deep, numbed grief.

Bill looked quickly away and for minutes on end forced himself to keep his mind a blank. He was presently startled by a restless murmur of sound running along the big room as the spectators, then the court, rose. John Updyke nudged his arm and he came erect, remaining so while the judge left the hall and entered his improvised chambers.

Bill noticed Updkye looking toward the jury now and, following his glance, saw the jurors waiting respectfully as Sam Akers' towering shape moved from the far end of the two rows of chairs and came this way. And a stir of resentment rose in him when Akers came abreast him and glanced his way briefly, sternly.

The hush that had held the big room was instantly broken as Akers' over-wide outline disappeared through the door of the small room that had been set aside for the jury's deliberations. Bill eyed Updyke then, and the lawyer told him, "The old boy forgot himself. The law doesn't tolerate the bench being that biased. We're asking that this be ruled a mistrial. Either that or we appeal."

"You're that sure of what the verdict will be?"

Updyke's thin face colored. "I didn't say that."

"But you meant it." A faint hope that had been in Bill Tenn died that moment.

Sam Akers was standing at the jury room's one grimy window looking down onto the mud-dirtied snow of the street as the last man came in and closed the door. He heard the lid of the stove bang, heard someone say, "Stoke 'er good, Jerry. It's killin' cold in here," and experienced a mild scorn of these townsmen and their need of creature comforts. To him the coolness of this room was refreshing, a relief after the stuffy staleness of the crowded, overheated hall outside.

"Well, Sam, let's take the vote and wind this up."

Akers turned, letting a studied impassivity settle over his face. Now was a critical moment, one in which he had decided he might add to his stature for being a generous, fair-minded man. Wanting to carry a certain point, he gruffly commented, "Let's not be too quick about this, Harvey. After all, a man's life is at stake here."

Harvey Ford, owner of the *Buena Vista*, had been poking at his stained teeth with a quill pick. His face went slack now in surprise. "Tenn was quick enough to take another man's. That's the devil of a way to talk, Sam. Don't you want to see Tenn swing for what he did to Buck?"

"I do if he's guilty."

"Guilty?" a second man echoed testily. "You mean you can doubt it? After the way he mauled Buck there on the street? He's a killer, take my word for it."

The speaker tongued a chew of tobacco from one cheek to the other, went on, "Akers, listen. Here's the simple facts, all that count. After the fight Buck went into the hotel bar, cuffed off a glass real quick like and headed home. He was killed on the way. Who by? By Tenn, who else? Now much as we admire your fairness, murder's never been tolerated among us."

Sam Akers smiled disarmingly, surveying these lesser men from his superior height. "Looks like I'm about the most unpopular cuss ever to set foot in court. First Updyke objecting to my servin' on the jury because of that set-to I had with Tenn, now —"

"The hell with Updyke." The man who had spoken noticed the way several others bridled at his remark and hastily amended it. "John's all right. But his objecting to you serving with us was just a lawyer's trick. You noticed Haldeman overruled him."

"Let's forget that and get to the point I'm trying to make," Akers said soberly. "There's a few holes in this case I don't like. One is what the old man had to say about going straight to their camp with Tenn and —"

"And the old coot was so much under the influence he couldn't have known where Tenn took him, or when."

Interrupted by Harvey Ford, whose word carried considerable weight, Akers lifted a hand and tried to school his expression to one of contriteness. "Sure, I know you got a point there. But, confound it, man, we've got no absolute proof that Tenn beat in the back of Buck's skull. According to law, a man on trial's got the benefit of any reasonable doubt. And I got what you might call that on a couple of counts."

The argument went on, Akers not joining in because he was relishing a deeply satisfying feeling of power at being able to sway these men's minds at will. He had stated his contrary views for only one reason, a devious one, believing that any man who shared them would find his position weakened at hearing the others attack it as an out and out absurdity. He had every intention of shortly backing down from the arbitrary stand he had taken, of letting Harvey Ford and the rest think they had brought him around to their way of thinking. In so doing he was certain that his example would forestall anyone else voting against Tenn's guilt.

He had planned this hours ago, seeing it as an effective way of increasing the respect these eleven men held for him. It had never occurred to him to take this stand as a means of saving an innocent man's life. Bill Tenn would hang, the Moguls wouldn't be hauled over the pass, his worries would be at an end. Buck Flynn's discovery, that rich vein of silver, was his now. His biggest worry, the chance that Buck might have told Sheila about him that night before he met the Irishman on the street, was also behind him. For over these two days he had caught Sheila's eye numerous times, and her smiles, the warmth of her glance, had told him that her liking for him hadn't weakened.

Sam Akers just now deeply relished a moment of looking back at what had happened three nights ago. The luck that had been with him so consistently all his adult years had been as strong then as he had ever known it. Following Buck at a distance after their argument, wondering how he was to handle that damning situation, he had seen the Irishman meet Tenn at the door of the *Buena Vista*, had seen the fight. And on the hunch that Buck would soon be returning home, he had waited there in the downstreet darkness.

No one had seen him. Hitting Buck, crushing in the back of the man's skull with a vicious downswing of his .44, had been as absurdly simple as on another occasion, long ago, when for a forgotten reason he had struck down another man the same way, a man whose name he could no longer recall.

"Damn it, Martinez! Who else could it have been?"

Harvey Ford's testy words intruded upon Akers' rumination. He saw Ford and two other jurors across by the stove scowling angrily at a slight dark-skinned man he remembered was the owner of a wood lot out Cedar Street.

Realizing that something unlooked-for had happened, he stepped over there just as Ford was growling, "But you got no more reason to talk that way than Sam here has."

Martinez glanced up at Akers in a pleading way. "You said it yourself, Mr. Akers. We don't have proof enough to hang him, do we?"

Clearing his throat to hide his startlement, Sam Akers stated noncommitally, "It bears some thinking on."

Martinez, a small and ordinarily retiring man, stretched to his full height now and, glaring at the others, told them, "I stand by my friend Mr. Akers here. I won't see you hang William Tenn. Put him away in prison, yes. For the rest of his life if you decide he's got it coming. But that's as far as I go."

Sam Akers was finally grasping the fact that he had somehow mismanaged this, that in taking his arbitrary stand of pointing out the weakness of the prosecution's case he had given this little man the courage to defy these others. He hadn't intended that, and now he found himself all but caught in his own trap.

For a moment he was experiencing the unsettling feeling that today things were unexpectedly working out for him much the same as they had the other day with Tenn, when his plan for buying the teams at a lower price had gone afoul. Though he realized all this, that both then and now his deviousness had worked against him, he wouldn't let himself consciously face the fact that a quirk of his nature was at fault.

Suddenly he saw something else. If the jury didn't bring in a verdict of Tenn being guilty of first degree murder, then sooner or later

Sheila would hear of his being the one mainly responsible for Buck's death being so weakly avenged. And with that thought upmost in mind he looked down at Martinez now to say, "I been standing here doing some thinking, my friend. Ford and these others may be right."

The little man's eyes showed shock and indignation. "How can you say that, Mr. Akers? You know they're wrong."

So the wrangling began again, Martinez growing even more positive in his stand and fighting these bigger men banty-fashion while Akers kept himself aloof from the argument.

It was Harvey Ford who finally decided things by growling, "The devil with this. We could stay here three more days and nights and get nowhere. Gents, we're licked. Tenn doesn't hang. We'll send him up for life and call it a day."

Someone else said, "Amen. But damned if I like it."

Akers could scarcely believe that eleven good men had given in to one of their number whose stature, until today, had been insignificant. Yet there it was. Martinez had won his point.

And as Harvy Ford began writing out the wording of the verdict, Sam Akers had to be satisfied with the knowledge that Bill Tenn was just as safely out of his way in prison as he would be if he was climbing a scaffold tomorrow at sunrise. Tenn's teams wouldn't be hauling Burgess's engines over the mountain.

Sheila Flynn sat in stunned bewilderment after Akers had announced the jury's decision and Judge Haldeman pounded the table to quiet the crowd's angry protest.

She heard John Updyke announce his intention of filing an appeal on the verdict, heard Haldeman sourly tell the lawyer that his intentions were no concern of this court. She listened as the judge sentenced William Tenn to spend the rest of his natural life in confinement at hard labor, and then watched the marshal and a deputy lead Tenn away.

After that, as Haldeman announced that the court was adjourned, and the hum of angry voices once again filled the big hall, her glance clung to Sam Akers. She was trying to decide something about him, something that abruptly prompted her to tell her mother, "Wait for me, mom," and rise from the hard bench to walk along the rail toward the jury box.

She caught Sam Akers' eye and gave him a nod that brought him toward her. Perhaps it was because she was over-wrought that she found his broad smile annoying. And when

When he was mad he'd either walk my legs off or swear the air blue. I'm too old for one any longer and you're too much of a lady for the other. So if you're bound to wear yourself out, go on ahead."

Sheila slowed her stride, smiling down in apology in a way that made Brigid Flynn all at once forget certain of her misgivings. She was proud of this daughter who, much like Buck, seemed to be so wholly Tim Flynn's offspring. Both of her children had inherited their father's tallness, his temper and merry disposition. Yet at times, particularly of late, she had suspected Sheila of maturing into a woman who could see beneath the surface of things, as she did herself but as neither Tim nor Buck ever had.

It had been a hard life but a full one for Brigid Flynn. Even now in the face of this tragedy she could never allow herself to regret having taken the long voyage across the Atlantic thirty years ago to marry a Boston carpenter. Nor could she regret Tim having become so fiddle-footed that he brought her into a new life, brought her on an emigrant train from Independence to this remote country.

Buck bringing home good pay had lately made the struggle running a boarding house less critical than it had been during her earlier nothing to do with right now, mom. Can't you see how unfair it all is?"

"I could if I'd let myself. But when you've reached my age you'll understand that stirring up your bile seldom changes things. It's done with."

"Maybe it isn't." Sheila nodded to the crowded walk across the street at the foot of the stairway leading to the marshal's office and the jail above Euler's shoe shop. "Maybe those men are mad enough to do something about it."

"No mob ever made anything right, honey."

Her mother's tone was so dispassionate that Sheila asked in wonder, "Don't you believe he deserves to hang?"

"Perhaps I do. But twelve men decided differently. We have to believe they were right."

"I won't believe it."

Shaking her head, Brigid Flynn said softly, "I won't either. Never."

Those positive words stayed with Sheila all the way to the house. And when her mother told her, "Think I'll go up and lie down a minute or two before we start supper," Sheila answered, "Yes. Let's eat late."

The girl went into the parlor and was on the point of lighting a lamp against the gathering dusk when she thought better of it and instead went to sit in the rocker by the front window and look out onto the snowy street. For the first minute or two as she heard her mother moving about in the upstairs front bedroom, her thoughts of the trial were confused. Yet once that sound had died away they became more rational, more orderly.

She discovered that Sam Akers having spoken for the jury angered her almost as much as his unconvincing denial of having approved of the verdict. It was an irrational feeling, she realized, for as foreman he had been required to read the verdict. Yet she had unaccountably sensed from his defensive words that he had had something to do with the verdict being what it was. How that had come about was beyond her understanding.

Two nights ago after Sam Akers had called here at the house she had found herself seriously trying to analyze her feelings toward him. She had even wondered if, at last, she might be beginning to love a man. Weeks ago she had been more in awe of Akers than anything else. But lately she had gathered that his intentions toward her were far from casual, in the light of which her regard for him had undergone a subtle change. Yet even now she couldn't define her feelings, for she had a strong sense of hardly knowing what he was really like, of his having let her see only the surface of his nature.

Presently her thoughts turned to John Updyke's final words. If he was filing an appeal there was a chance that Tenn might not serve out all of his sentence. Perhaps a rehearing might even mean his being set free altogether.

Judges, juries and lawyers were hardly to be trusted in these days of loose law enforcement that saw known criminals roaming the Territory, free either because of unfair trial or because peace officers lacked the will or the courage to make arrests. She excluded John Updyke from this indictment, for he was an old friend and had doubtless acted according to his convictions in defending Tenn. Even so, because of Updyke there was probably an even chance that Tenn would eventually join the ranks of other criminals at large.

Looking back over one interval there this afternoon, she found herself deeply ashamed. She had been furtively observing Tenn and had caught herself wondering how a murderer's instincts could be so well hidden in such a clean looking, even handsome man. For a moment her resolve to hate him had come close to weakening.

But now it was stronger than ever. She despised William Tenn with a passion that was almost frightening. Buck had been a fine man, worthy of the fierce pride and love she held for him. The man who had struck him down was beneath contempt.

Convinced of this, believing without a trace of doubt that justice had fallen far short of righting a wrong today, Sheila Flynn reached a grave decision as she sat there in the dying light.

It took her all of a quarter-hour to think out what she was to do, to convince herself of its rightness. At the end of that interval she rose from the chair and moved soundlessly from the room to tiptoe upstairs.

She was thankful at finding the door to her mother's room shut. She moved back along the hallway to Buck's room as stealthily as she could, turned the door's knob and pushed the panel slowly open.

There was barely enough light to let her make her way hesitantly to the far wall where she knew Buck's holster and shell-belt hung under the wool coat he would never wear again.

She lifted the heavy Colt's from its worn leather sheath, looking down at it bleakly a long moment before opening the loading gate, drawing back the hammer and rolling the cylinder to count five dull brass shell casings.

Fred Stone was cold and, hands thrust deep in overcoat pockets, kept stamping his feet against the walk's packed snow as he waited in front of the *Buena Vista* for the late afternoon eastbound, due over the pass from Granite at five o'clock but already late.

He stood apart from a group of eight or ten others who were here to meet the stage. In his twenty minutes of waiting he had spoken to only two passersby. Though he was inconspicuous and appeared uninterested in what was going on around him, he was taking it all in.

Once when two youngsters, hitching a ride on their sled behind a buckboard, rolled into the snow as the rig turned sharply into the cross street, Stone smiled sparely to join the laughter of the nearby group. Another time, though he didn't appear to be listening, he paid strict attention to three men standing at the foot of the hotel steps arguing the niceties of building a proper gallows, one that would drop the condemned man far enough to end his suffering quickly, yet not far enough to risk the snapping of the rope.

Their discussion had been prompted by one man complaining bitterly about the outcome of the trial half an hour ago. Fred Stone had attended only the final session this afternoon, so wasn't too well informed on what had gone on before. The jury's verdict had brought him a keen disappointment. He had liked Buck

71

Flynn, yet he had also liked what he had seen of the stranger, Bill Tenn.

In his discerning way it struck him as incongruous that Tenn, having licked Flynn in a brawl, should want to kill him. It was because he didn't believe Tenn to be a killer, and because he couldn't believe justice had been done, that he was waiting here now.

When the stage did appear out of the gathering dusk, throwing chunks of caked snow from its high wheel rims, Stone at once saw the reason for its being late. The near lead horse, a bay, was limping badly. And as the high Concord swayed to a stop at the walk's edge he plainly heard the driver threaten the Granite yard man with bodily harm for having done such a poor job of shoeing the animal.

Mary Stone was the second passenger to alight from the coach. Starting toward his daughter, an inner warmth was ridding Stone of his chill and of the trial's bad aftertaste. Mary abruptly saw him there at the back edge of the group and her eyes brightened with delight as she came to him.

"Dad, I didn't expect you'd be here." She kissed him lightly on the cheek, took his arm and led him over to where a man from the hotel was taking the luggage the driver was throwing down from the boot.

She handed Stone her wicker suitcase, carrying a hat-box herself as they left the group and started up the walk. "It worked out just the way you said it would," she told him excitedly, "staying three days instead of only one. I gave Mrs. Burke her fitting and finished the dress. Then she asked if I couldn't stay the night with them and do over one of her coats the next day. When I told her I'd planned on staying anyway she had two other women in. And today three more. I've got a month's work ahead of me."

"Fine, fine." Stone spoke with his usual gravity, though she could tell by his eyes that he was really pleased. "This ought to mean we can get you the new machine."

"Not only that, but I can go to Granite two days a month from now on for fittings and new orders." She squeezed his arm. "Dad, I'm really in business. If it keeps on, I'll have to hire a seamstress to help me."

She saw that he was only half listening now and, wondering at his preoccupation, suddenly remembered something. "The trial. How did it come out?"

"They're putting Tenn away for life."

"Only that?" Mary was plainly disappointed. "But I thought they had him dead to rights."

"No." Stone shook his head, adding quite deliberately, "There was a lot about the trial to leave a man wondering. That is, if he took the time to think." He looked around at her. "Which is one of the reasons I came to meet you."

At her look of puzzlement, he told her, "I want you to go to John Updyke. Tonight. Right now."

"But, dad. All I —"

"It isn't much, probably doesn't mean a thing. But I think he should be told what you know."

They had unconsciously been walking slower, and now Mary stopped, her look grave. "You think Tenn was innocent?"

"Almost, Mary. But you won't find many others who'd agree with me. There was considerable feeling when the jury didn't recommend hanging." Fred Stone was a man with a conscience, though the past three years of keeping Sam Akers' accounts had put considerable strain on it. Sometimes, looking back as he had this past hour and wondering at the circumstances that had made him continue working for a man whose principles were so at odds with his own, he would begin to doubt himself.

Yet he had remained a strictly honest man despite the taint of the many instances of Akers' dishonesty he kept filed away in his orderly mind. Just now, since what he was asking of Mary was so closely linked with Akers, he was aware that he was taking a certain risk. But he had thought it out carefully, deciding the risk had to be taken if he was to rid himself of a certain nagging doubt that had unsettled his peace of mind since the morning after Buck had died, the morning on which Mary had taken the early stage across the pass.

Mary, studying him in the fading light, saw that he was really troubled. And in her forthright way, believing implicitly that anything he did was right, she told him, "If you think it's the thing to do, I'll go."

Stone gave her one of his rare smiles, reaching out to take the hat-box. "Supper'll be ready by the time you're back. Hope you won't mind my cooking."

"You're the best cook I know."

She was turning away when he told her, "There was a light in Updyke's office just now. If he isn't there, you'll probably find him at home. His is the house —"

"I know the one."

"One other thing, Mary." He waited until she looked around at him. "Just to avoid any unpleasantness, don't mention that this was my notion. But you needn't lie about it if he asks you. You've been away, you just now got back and heard how the trial came out.

This thing's been on your mind and you just
. . . you don't think it's important, but you
want him to have all the facts."

Mary seldom heard her father speak at such
length and, with womanly intuition, quietly
asked, "It is important, isn't it, dad?"

"That's for John Updyke to judge. By the
way, you know him, know what he looks
like?"

"Of course. Thin and with nice blue eyes
and —"

"Then hustle. We have a lot to talk over."

Mary was vaguely troubled as she went back
down the walk, picking her way carefully
along one unshovelled stretch where the fail-
ing light made it hard to follow the narrow,
packed pathway. Her first real jubilation over
having come home with the means for bol-
stering the family finances was gone now as
she sensed the importance her father attached
to her errand.

She wondered why this couldn't have waited
until morning. But by the time she was crossing the street at the hotel corner and could
see the men loafing on the walk below the
marshal's office further on, she had her first
inkling of the tensions that must have been
gripping Pinetop these past three days. That
awareness made her gather her coat more
tightly about her and hurry on.

Approaching John Updyke's lighted office window, she experienced an odd embarrassment overlaid by an emotion akin to eagerness. She had never met John Updyke. She had first noticed him in church one Sunday morning perhaps three months ago when he had been sitting in a pew obliquely in front of her. As she listened to the sermon she had discovered herself studying his angular near-gaunt face. And she had begun wondering what there was about his homeliness that made her know he must be a man of considerable intelligence and understanding.

Later, after the service as she joined the crowd in the aisle directly behind him, she had noticed the number of people who spoke to him or made a point of shaking his hand. And because his shy yet genuinely warm manner impressed her, she had asked about him.

That distant encounter with John Updyke had been the first of several, all equally distant. At the last session of court she had made it a point to attend a bankruptcy hearing where he was representing the defendant. She had come to know the sound of his voice, his lucid and alert manner of speaking. Above all, she had come to know that he tempered a startling keenness of mind with a wry sense of humor.

There had never been a particular reason for analyzing her interest in John Updyke, or even for seeing it as anything but common-place. And just now as she approached his door she was aware only of looking forward to her first meeting with the man.

As Mary Stone came into his office, John Updyke laid down a pen and rose quickly from the chair at his desk. Though he was startled at seeing who his visitor was, his eyes showed instant recognition.

Before he could speak, Mary asked hesitantly, "Is this the wrong time to be coming here?"

"It's exactly the right time, Miss Stone." He had been working in shirtsleeves, and now took his coat from the back of the chair and pulled it on, nodding down to the disorder of his desk. "I've about bogged down on this. Here, take this chair." He came around and pulled a big leather armchair well into the light of the desk's green-shaded lamp.

"So you know who I am?"

"Indeed. Fred Stone's your father. According to rumor, you do things with thread and yard goods the likes of which have never before been seen around here."

"You exaggerate, Mr. Updyke." Mary laughed, knowing that the compliment was genuine. And as she took the chair she told him, "I promise not to take much of your time."

"That's to be regretted." Letting his spare frame down into the chair behind the desk once more, he was feeling an abrupt easing of the day-long depression and disappointment. Mary Stone's presence made this sparsely furnished room seem less drab and gave him something other than Bill Tenn's insecure future to think about.

This girl was small and delicate looking. Yet her eyes betrayed a merriness and a vivacity that spoke as certainly of high spirits and good health as did the quick, purposeful way she moved. He had seen her many times on the street these past weeks and, liking her looks, had long ago made it a point of finding out who she was.

He reached for his pipe just now, arching his brows in a silent query that made her say, "Yes, do. I like the smell of pipe tobacco."

He packed the briar and, about to hold a lighted match over the bowl, motioned to the papers before him. "If you ever have a son, Miss Stone, don't let him follow the law."

"What is it you're doing?"

"Drafting an appeal on the trial today."

"That's the reason I'm here." When his glance lifted sharply, Mary added, "Not the real reason, perhaps. But it has to do with Buck Flynn."

She went on to explain that she had been

away, and before she realized it the nervousness and self-consciousness had left her and she was speaking straightforwardly, reassured by his calm attentiveness.

". . . Then when I heard how the trial had gone, I began thinking you should know of something that happened the night before I left. The night Buck was killed."

"Something you saw?"

"Heard more than saw. I was taking Mrs. Torens a shirt-waist I knew she'd be needing before I got back. On the way I heard two men arguing across the street. Worse than arguing, I think, because —"

"What time was this, Miss Stone?"

"After seven. Nearly half-past, long after dark."

He nodded, striking another match now and his thin cheeks moving in and out as he drew the pipe alight. "Go on."

"I knew Buck Flynn well enough to recognize his voice. And I've been to dad's office often enough to know the sound of Mr. Akers', too."

The abrupt way John Updyke's look changed from one of polite interest to one of faint excitement let Mary know that what she was telling him might not be so trivial after all. A moment ago she had been wishing she hadn't come here. Yet now she was glad she had as she went on, "They were there in front of the house. From the way they were talking I could tell that Buck was mad, really mad. Mr. Akers was just like he always is, not raising his voice. It sounded like he was trying to calm Buck."

The lawyer drew deeply on the pipe, blew the smoke ceilingward. "Hear anything they said, anything in particular?"

Mary started to shake her head, but then answered, "I do. Yet it's . . . I've had so little time to think about it that I'd like to be sure of something before I tell you what it was. In a way, what I remember is hard to believe. Could you . . . could I have time to think about it before I try and tell you?"

He was puzzled, yet nevertheless nodded. "Of course."

"One thing I can say now. They must have heard me when I was right opposite them. Because Buck all at once dropped his voice. It was embarrassing to know he'd heard me."

"They were the ones to be embarrassed." Updyke was eyeing her closely. "Does your father know about this?"

When she nodded reluctantly, he put another question. "He sent you to me?"

Again, she answered reluctantly and only after deciding to follow her instinct for trusting this man. "Yes. But he's not to know I've told you."

"He won't. You have my word."

"Could this . . . Sheila's one of the closest friends I've made since coming here. And I was fond of Buck. But it . . . it seems dad almost thinks Tenn isn't guilty. Could this possibly help him?"

The lawyer smiled crookedly. "It'll depend on what you remember, Mary. So far it's blessed little to go on." His glance betrayed a momentary embarrassment at having called her by name and he hurried on to say, "Bill would want me to thank you for trying to help."

"I want to help."

Mary was relieved that he wasn't pressing her for a further explanation, though now as she rose, deciding there was little point in remaining longer, she thought of something that gave her a troubled look. And as he hurried across to open the door for her she told him, "I haven't had the chance of seeing Sheila and her mother. I suppose now's as good a time as any to call."

"It might upset them if you repeat what you've just told me."

"I know. I won't mention it."

She looked up and smiled as he opened the door. And as he felt the piercing chill of the evening air strike him she asked, "You don't think I'm being unfair, wanting to be sure of this before I say anything?"

Updyke shook his head. "No. I'd rather have it this way than have you be mistaken. Could I . . . Would you mind my coming to see you in a day or two when you've had time to think it over?"

"Of course not. You're welcome at the house any time you'd like to come."

He nodded gratefully. "Good night. And my regards to your father."

Watching Mary Stone go on along the walk, breathing deeply as he caught a lingering trace of the light scent she wore, John Updyke was feeling a stronger awareness of this girl's attractiveness than he was of the unlooked-for word she had brought him. But then as he shut the door and sauntered back to his desk to stare down at a sheet of paper lined with his even, open handwriting, he did begin thinking of what she had told him. He was presently stifling a hope, telling himself *No two men ever worked together but what they tangled now and then.*

Yet there remained the bald fact that Akers and Buck Flynn had quarreled the night Buck died and that, so far as he knew, Sam Akers had told no one of having seen his foreman after the closing of the office. That in itself was to be wondered at.

Taking a heavy gold watch from his vest

pocket, he saw that it was nearly six o'clock. Bill Tenn must right now be eating his supper, and probably not relishing it. And with the thought, *Maybe I can cheer him up,* the lawyer went to the coatrack near the door, took down his heavy overcoat and shrugged into it.

In another minute he was down the street approaching a small group of men gathered near the stairway climbing to the marshal's office and the jail above Euler's shoe shop. He nodded to them and was reaching out for a hold on the stair rail when someone said, "Lay you even money we'll have him strung up by morning."

Updyke halted, slowly turning, peering into the darkness trying to recognize these men. "You've made yourself a bet, whoever you are. For fifty dollars. Or a hundred if you want." He reached inside his coat and brought out a long, flat wallet which, in fact, was empty except for some papers. "Let's see the color of your money."

No one moved or spoke, and after waiting out a deliberate interval Updyke said sharply, "Come on, show your face and put up."

His eyes were becoming accustomed to the darkness and now he thought he recognized two of the men. What he knew of them put an edge of scorn to his tone when, still getting no response, he told them, "I'm bringing blankets up here after supper. Blankets and a ten bore. If any of you are so inclined, we'll try and work up some business for Bert Travers."

He turned and climbed the stairway, really worried now, wondering if tomorrow would in fact be a full day for the coroner whose name he had mentioned so casually.

He found Red Bushrod, the marshal, sitting in a chair tilted against the wall, an oily rag in hand and polishing a Henry rifle lying across his knees. Bushrod had gripped the rifle with both hands at the sound of the door opening. But when he saw who it was he relaxed and resumed his chore after a brief nod.

Closing the door, Updyke said, "Company down below, Red."

"So I notice. 'Most every tramp in town."

"Could be the beginning of something."

"Suppose it could." Bushrod sighed resignedly. "And to think where I'd be right now if I hadn't taken this fool job. Workin' the place for old Catlett up on the Squaw. Nothing to do but put in an easy day, and of an evening watch that Nancy girl swing her skirts and give me the come-on with her eyes. Hell, why did I listen to these old coots when they told me how good I'd look behind a badge?"

"We all make mistakes, Red." The lawyer nodded toward the street. "What do we do about it?"

"Me? Get myself a pot of coffee and try and stay awake till sun-up with old Nelly here for company." The marshal affectionately stroked the scarred stock of the Henry.

John Updyke was frowning in thought and now sauntered across to peer into the darkness beyond the upstreet-facing window opposite the stairway door. The rutted snow by the intersection was lighted feebly by the hotel veranda lamps and he saw a pair of men cross from the far walk and head this way. Across four intervening snow-whitened roofs more lights cut the blackness, shining from three of the *Buena Vista*'s upstair's windows.

Apparently the town was quiet. But he hadn't liked the look of those two men heading in the direction of the group below, and on sudden impulse he turned to the marshal. "Tell you what. I'll round up four good men. We'll put two in the alley out back, two in front. We'll get fires going both places. To keep warm by and to see by, just in case. Then I'll come up here and take you on at a game of cribbage to pass the time."

Bushrod considered this deliberately, his pride struggling against his common sense. Finally he settled on a compromise and shrugged. "He's your client, John. Do whatever you want."

Updyke nodded to the bolt-studded door

86

at the room's rear. "Mind if I have a word with him?"

"After she's finished."

"She?"

"Oh, forgot to mention it. Buck's sister is in there with him."

The lawyer's eyes came wider open in sharp surprise. "Sheila? When did this happen?"

"About a minute before you come in."

"Did she say what she wanted of him?"

"Nope. Didn't ask. I . . . it did seem sort of out of line, her wanting to talk to the man who done Buck in. But Sheila's not the one to take no for an answer. So when she said she wanted to see him in private, I locked her in with him like I do when you come to see him. Was it wrong?"

"No," the lawyer answered hesitantly. "From the sound of it you didn't have much choice."

"Seems to me the council could vote some money to fix up a real jail, John. Or at least run some bars across in there and leave a sort of alleyway so's anyone wanting to see a prisoner wouldn't be right in the lock-up with him."

Updyke nodded absent-mindedly, staring at the jail door, wondering if he should go in there. But finally he decided against it, thinking that in another hour he would after all be seeing Bill and discovering the reason for Sheila Flynn's unlooked-for visit.

He was hungry now and, realizing he hadn't eaten since morning, went to the stairway door. "Give me an hour to get things set and to eat, Red. Sit tight."

"Nothing much else to do."

Once the marshal had padlocked the steel-barred inner door and swung the outer one shut, not bolting it, Sheila Flynn leaned back against the wall and for the first time eyed Bill Tenn squarely. When she had first glimpsed him he had been lying with blond head pillowed on a wadded blanket at the near end of the cell's single bunk along the back wall. Now he was standing, eyeing her with a disconcerting directness.

He abruptly moved out from the bunk, the cell's only furnishing except for a small sheet-metal stove, a wood box and a lantern hanging on the far side of the door. "Care to sit down?"

She remained motionless, not answering, holding her knit wool muff tightly against the belt of her narrow-waisted coat. Her right hand, gripping the handle of Buck's Colt's, felt chill, clammy. And as the weight of Tenn's glance met hers and she saw no remorse or even embarrassment in his eyes, she was suddenly furious, glad that she had come here to kill him.

"You're not the least bit ashamed, are you?"

"Yes," came his surprising answer. "Ashamed of having you think I should be."

Sheila's tone was edged with loathing as she retorted, "Still playing the innocent, are you?"

"Look, Miss Flynn. This isn't doing either of us any good. If it's your reason for being here, why not call it quits and leave?"

"But I have another reason for being here."

He tried and failed to understand what her words meant, yet the gleam of satisfaction in her green eyes told him she wasn't speaking idly. For a moment he had the hope that she was here for some reason other than to torment him. Yet that hope was shortlived, for abruptly she was asking,

"What did you do, wait there on the street behind a tree and club him when he came past you?"

This time it was his turn to ignore her. He eased down onto the foot of the bunk, took tobacco from pocket and began building a smoke, not looking at his hands but at her. He shortly saw that she was about to speak again. But then she all at once half turned toward the door, and the next moment he was hearing voices sounding faintly from the marshal's office beyond.

She turned slowly to face him once more.

"There are one or two things I want you to know before . . ." she checked her words momentarily. "What you've done leaves mother and me alone. Perhaps you know we take in boarders. They never did bring us quite enough to live on. Buck has been making up the difference out of his pay."

Bill drew on the cigarette, exhaling with a sigh.

When he didn't speak, she went on, "I want you to know this and think about it while you're still able."

He looked across at her with a frown. "Able?"

At first it seemed she hadn't heard him, for her glance had strayed to the bars beside her again as the muffled sound of a door closing came from Bushrod's office. She appeared to be relieved then as she looked around at him once more. "Yes. Able to think. Or even to breathe."

For a scant second her words made not the slightest sense to him. But then he saw her draw her right hand from the muff held tight against her waist, saw the .44 Colt's swing around in line with him. And suddenly what she had said took on sharp meaning.

"You're going to die, Bill Tenn." Sheila's voice was hushed, hollow with emotion. "You'll know how Buck felt. Only I hope you'll feel it longer than he did."

He dropped the cigarette to the floor. As an afterthought he ground it under the sole of his boot, his glance not straying from the girl or from the big bore of the Colt's.

Some of the color had left Sheila's face and he had the odd experience of being disturbed by a sudden awareness of her exquisite beauty. But then his thoughts steadied and he told himself, *She'll really do it. Say something.* Yet when he groped for words they wouldn't come. And in another moment she was asking, "Aren't you going to beg? Aren't you going to tell me I'm wrong, that you didn't kill him?"

"Would it make any difference if I did?"

"Not the slightest.'"

Her words somehow lacked conviction. He could see the gun waver slightly, could see the beginning of uncertainty in her eyes. And because he sensed that her nerves were drawn almost to the breaking point, he came slowly up off the bunk, telling her, "You'll always wonder, won't you? And if you should stumble on the truth of how it really happened, you'll never be able to shake it. You'll think of it by day and dream of it at night, the nights you can sleep."

Sheila Flynn shook her head violently, as though closing her mind to the awesome possibility that she might be wrong about this. "No." A momentary uncertainty faded from her eyes and they once more reflected hate, loathing. "I'll think back and be —"

He whipped the blanket from the straw mattress and threw it at her, wheeling hard aside and then lunging toward her. The blanket struck her full in the face, furling heavily down over her head and shoulders. He was almost within arm-reach of her when the Colt's exploded deafeningly, the blast pushing the blanket outward.

Bill struck at the bulge of the weapon and the .44 thudded to the floor almost at his feet. Sheila was clawing at the blanket as he reached out, put an arm about her waist and snatched up the gun.

A chair banged the floor in the marshal's office. Holding the struggling girl, pinning her arms to her sides and hearing her choked cry, Bill swung around so that he squarely faced the door. He put the muzzle of the Colt's against the padlock, thumbed back the hammer and squeezed trigger.

He saw the padlock blown apart as the gun's thunderclap burst across the cell. And now he suddenly let go his hold on Sheila, reached out and pulled the barred door wide.

The heavy plank panel beyond was swinging back and he lunged straight at it, hitting it with his shoulder. It moved back another foot, then jolted him viciously as it collided with something. He fell to his knees, seeing Red Bushrod sprawl to the office floor close beyond. He dove at the man.

The marshal had managed to roll halfway over and was lifting a gun trying to line it, when Bill's arcing .44 smashed in at his temple. The man's frame went limp, and Bill lunged erect.

Boots pounded on the stairway outside and he wheeled across the room to throw the bolt on the door. His coat and hat hung where he had left them on returning from the trial this afternoon. He yanked them from their hook, ran to the room's side window and threw up its lower sash.

It was a four foot drop to the adjoining roof, and as he jumped, hearing the scrape of boots in the room behind him, he was pulling on his coat. Suddenly a shadow blocked out the pale rectangle of light the window laid across the snowy roof. Turning, he saw Bushrod standing there lining a gun down at him. He let himself fall sideways, the weapon above thundering out across the night, its echo slamming back from the hotel wall.

Bill ran back along the slope of the roof, nearly falling once as his boots slipped against the snow. He halted sharply as the pitch blackness was about to let him carry himself off into space at the roof's rear edge. Looking downward, he could make out nothing of what lay below along the alley.

But then a second explosion behind him, and the sound of a bullet droning away in a ricochette, warned him he was running out of time. He threw himself outward into the empty blackness of the night.

III

The staccato pound of the two shots Bushrod fired at Bill Tenn's indistinct shape fading back along the neighboring roof rolled out across the night to lay an instant tension through the town.

Fred Stone, wearing a flour-sacking apron and about to stir the fire in his kitchen stove, stiffened at the sound and held the lid-lifter motionless, wondering why Mary should be so late and faintly worrying about her. Brigid Flynn, standing on her porch saying goodbye to Mary after their tearful words about Buck, pulled a shawl together across her shoulders and tried to believe that the shots didn't necessarily mean trouble.

Three men loafing beside the iced-over iron watering trough in front of the hotel turned sharply as the explosions rolled along the street, then ran down the walk. Two others, the remnant of the group that had earlier gathered below the marshal's office, stood undecided a moment staring warily upward at the light in the marshal's office window. Then they lunged for the stairway. And John Updyke, on his way into a restaurant far up the street caught his breath, wheeled and ran out into the rutted snow in the direction of the jail.

That second thunderclap blast of Bushrod's gun had deafened Sheila, turned her rigid with stark apprehension. She faintly heard the marshal growl, "Damn," and afterward leaned against the jail door, an unlooked-for and startling thankfulness leaving her all at once weak.

The marshal turned from the window, letting the smoking gun drop to his side. "Didn't even come close."

For a moment he eyed Sheila quizzically, as though reading her dread and sudden awareness of almost having caused a man to die tonight. But then as he pulled a handkerchief from pocket and gingerly pressed it to the side of his aching, bleeding scalp she knew he was too miserable and befuddled to be thinking of anyone or anything but himself.

The thud of boots sounded from the stairway outside now, and as someone began pounding the bolted door Bushrod bawled, "Wait." He had started across there when all at once the panel was forced and slammed back into the wall.

Two men burst into the office, halting sharply at sight of the marshal standing with gun in hand. He eyed the pair stonily, drawling, "Nice work. Go ahead, tear the place apart."

"Lord, Red. We thought you were in trouble. What happened?"

Bushrod ignored them, his glance swinging abruptly to Sheila. "Just what went on in there, Sheila? Had someone passed him that —"

"Can't we talk about it later?" she cut in, closing her eyes and shaking her head as though wanting to rid herself of some unpleasant thought.

"Guess we can." . . . The marshal sighed in frustration and pain. "You better be getting on home."

The men by the door moved aside as Sheila came toward them. And Bushrod, noticing her dazed look and the faltering way in which she moved, asked gently, "You all right? Did he rough you up?"

Sheila only now realized that in pulling away the blanket she had mussed her hair. She paused, reaching up and brushing several lose strands of hair from her forehead. "No, he didn't," she said quickly. "He was . . . he didn't even touch me."

She heard more men coming up the stairway now and hurried out of the room. And Bushrod, worried about her, breathed, "A damned sweet mess for a girl like that to run into."

"What happened, Red?"

"What happened? Hell, can't you see?" The marshal waved his gun at the open jail door. "Tenn's gone is what happened."

"Gone how?"

Bushrod swore. "Don't ask me how when I don't know how myself yet."

Three more men came into the room now, followed closely by five others, then still another. Everyone was talking at once, asking questions, giving meaningless answers. And as John Updyke shortly pushed his way in through the door, Red Bushrod's throbbing head drove him to losing all patience.

"All right, half you jokers clear out," he called. "And don't jam the stairs or the fool thing'll cave in."

Two or three of the most recent arrivals reluctantly went on out. It was Updyke who finally managed to push the door shut and lean back against it.

That was the signal for the marshal to scan his packed office and say tartly, "Tenn's got away. How, we don't know yet. But he's gone. Out this window and by way of the alley. Now I want to find out a couple things and find 'em fast. Len, you hike on back there with a lantern and have a look, see which way he went. Hiram, get on out to the fire house and sound the bell. The rest of you spread along the street and try and spot him."

Pausing, he studied the faces before him. "Now all of you clear out and be back at the horse barn in five minutes." As an afterthought, he added, "All but you, Updyke."

The room emptied quickly. And when John Updyke had closed the door once again, Bushrod fixed him with a baleful stare. "How did you pass it to him, John?"

"Pass what?"

"The gun. How did you get it in there to Tenn?"

The lawyer's brows arched in surprise. "He had a gun?"

"Look," the marshal breathed wearily, impatiently. "I'm dry behind the ears. Tenn shot the lock off the inside door. He belted me with his iron on the way out. I want to know how you got it to him."

"You've searched me every time I've gone in there, Red. He didn't get any gun from me."

"I've got your word on that?"

At Updyke's nod, Bushrod shook his head in a baffled way. "Then it must've been Sheila."

The lawyer's look was startled, puzzled. "Sheila? Why would she want to —"

"Don't ask me, but she's the only one besides you I've let in to see him. And you can damn' well bet she's going to answer for what she's done."

Bushrod turned angrily away now to the rack of rifles and shotguns behind his desk, lifting down the big Henry. And John Updyke picked this moment to open the door and say, "He's innocent, Red. If you kill him getting him back here you'll be killing a man who doesn't deserve to die."

The law man wheeled around. "After the way he pole-axed me, should I care if we bring him in on a plank?"

John Updyke shrugged and went on out, leaving Bushrod with the feeling that he had somehow put himself in the wrong, though he didn't quite know how or why.

He was hoping he had seen the last of the lawyer tonight. Yet in two more minutes when he went on down to the street and obliquely across it to the livery barn, he found Updyke among the thirty or forty men waiting there, one of the dozen or so already mounted and ready to ride. The lawyer had changed from his long overcoat and was wearing a worn and dirty sheepskin, obviously borrowed.

Bushrod ignored him as men crowded around, several trying to speak at once. He held up a hand to silence them, calling loudly, "One at a time. Len Ewing was going to have a look at the alley. Is he back yet?"

"Right here, Red. Found where he jumped off Crippen's roof and lit on a pile of ashes. Looks like he took one sweet spill. He made off up the alley limpin' badly, from the looks of his tracks. Then I lost him there along Cedar where the walks've been shovelled."

"Who else knows anything?"

A man holding a lantern lifted it so that its light let the marshal make out several more faces. "Elvin Pike thinks he saw him crossing Cedar there above the feed store," this one said. "He isn't quite —"

The speaker broke off now as the slow, deep-toned notes of the fire bell rolled sonorously down the street. Bushrod breathed a low oath, knowing he had enough men here to form a posse and wishing now he hadn't thought of this way of further arousing the town.

Abruptly impatient to be away from here before the crowd thickened, he asked, "Is that all? No one else knows anything?"

"Here comes something, maybe," a man alongside him said.

Bushrod followed his glance, seeing a man running this way along the near plank walk. In several more seconds the newcomer came lumbering in on the group, so badly winded he had considerable difficulty blurting out, "Red, he got . . . got away on a horse. That

chestnut of . . . Pryor's from right in front
of —"

"Which way?" Bushrod cut in.

"South toward Akers' camp."

"His own camp, you mean," someone said.
"Let's go."

The marshal called sharply, "Hold on. We
do this right." He eyed the man who had
brought the news. "How long ago was this,
Henry?"

"Must've been all of ten minutes from what
I make out."

"Then he's on his way." Bushrod was having trouble unsnarling his thoughts but in another moment spoke loudly, so that all these
men could hear. "A couple of you get up
above, light a fire and block the pass road.
A couple more had better circle out beyond
the tunnel camp to cut him off if he heads
south. The rest of us'll go pay a visit on that
old hardboot looking after his horses. Now
hold on."

"Hold on? Why? He's gettin' away."

Bushrod scowled at the speaker. "Listen,
all of you. It'd be nice to bring this cuss in
without no holes in him. But I want him back
even if you got to make a gravel sifter out
of him. So any man without iron better stick
close to someone with." He noticed Updyke
peering down at him, looked the other way

102

as he called his final word. "Work in pairs when we split up. And I don't want no more than twenty men altogether."

He pushed on through the crowd and up the livery barn's ramp, hurrying into the stable to get his gelding, irritated at this delay, at no one having thought to saddle up for him. And presently as the posse lined out at a fast jog up the street he was careful to avoid riding anywhere near Updyke.

He halted the group at the intersection of Cedar Street long enough to single out four men, not two as he had first said, who were to ride up the pass road. And in five more minutes, with fully thirty riders strung out behind him, he rode in on Early Jordan's lean-to near the brushed-in mouth of the small box canyon well below the fires of Sam Akers' work camp.

They found Jordan atop a stack of hay beyond his lean-to and fire, forking the sweet-smelling timothy over a long pile of oak-brush, feeding Bill Tenn's teams. And as they spread out on either side of the blaze and the improvised canvas lean-to, the old man jabbed his pitchfork into the hay and leaned on it, idly observing Bushrod as he approached.

"Well, out with it," the law man began gruffly. "Where did he go?"

Jordan looked down at him impassively.

"You been drinkin', marshal? Or do I try and guess what you're talking about?"

"Tenn has busted jail," Bushrod told him impatiently. "We think he —"

"Now that's just dandy." It was a plain statement of fact, the words holding no trace of surprise. "You want I should go along with you to look for him?"

The marshal sensed that he was gaining little by arguing, sensed also that Tenn had been here. So he motioned toward the lean-to, saying tartly, "One of you see if Tenn's saddle is gone. Len, you're good at reading sign. Get down and look around. We may be able to track him if he's been here."

Early Jordan reached up and pushed his wide hat to the back of his head, soberly observing, "Reminds me of a night I once tried trackin' in the snow, marshal. I was in a hurry to catch up with a colt that'd busted out of a pen at a line camp. Know what good it did me?"

"No. What?" Bushrod had no sooner spoken than he was regretting it, suspecting he was being baited.

"I'd made maybe three miles when it began to get light. Hoofed it most of the way because in the dark you can't see to track from the saddle. When it did get light, guess what I found out."

The marshal knew others were listening and snapped in irritation, "Go on, finish it. We don't have all night."

"Well, sir, come first light I found I'd lost the colt's sign somewhere back a ways and was following elk tracks. Then guess what happened."

Someone behind Bushrod chuckled softly. With a look of absolute seriousness Early Jordan went on, "I looked off along the line of that sign and, so help me, there come a big bull elk walking straight at me. Big as a house, he was. Here I was, afoot and leading my mare. She spotted the bull about the same time I did. Rared back, jerked the ribbons away and took off. Me, I took off right with her. Only I made for the nearest tree. Got there, too. But then guess what happened."

Several men were laughing now, and the angry way Bushrod looked around at them only made them laugh harder. Then in another moment someone was calling, "Come on, old timer. Then what happened?"

Early Jordan waited until he could be heard. "Spent half the fool day up that tree with the bull pawing the snow down below, me pegging sticks at him. Along about noon he lost interest and wandered off. I hoofed it back to the shack, near done in when I got there." . . . He tilted his head, eyeing the marshal with a poker face . . . "Now there's the reason I never track in the dark no more."

"You've wasted us about five minutes with that trumped up story," Bushrod growled.

The old man nodded sagely. "Come to think of it, I have."

The law man reined angrily away now, calling in sharp annoyance, "Move, some of you. Spread out and look for sign."

"This snow around here's cut up with so many tracks you won't have much luck," Jordan called, but if Bushrod heard he ignored the words.

The old man knelt and slid down off the stack now. Looking around he happened to see John Updyke sitting a bay horse nearby. The lawyer, intercepting his glance and not at all understanding the spare way he nodded, brought his animal across to him, saying tiredly, "Looks bad, Early."

"Bad? Hell, it looks good. He got away, didn't he?"

Early Jordan glanced on past Updyke to see where the others were. They had scattered, with the nearest man a good thirty feet distant. Still looking beyond the lawyer, he very softly said, "You could do worse than to be here come morning to help me shag Bill's nags across to Granite, lawyer. Say around seven o'clock."

Suddenly stiffening, he called sharply, "Hey, you with the sticky paws."

Without a further glance at Updyke, he hobbled away toward the lean-to where one of the posse had just reached down, picked up a blanket and tossed it aside.

"Think you'll find him buried in the snow under there, fella?" Jordan asked querulously. "Now clear out and leave my things be."

On leaving the marshal's office twenty minutes ago, Sheila had no sooner pushed her way past the men crowding the stairway and the walk below than she began feeling the aftereffects of those tense minutes in the jail. She found herself trembling as though in the grip of a hard chill, and tears unaccountably came to her eyes as she hurried along the walk.

Now that she had her first chance of looking back and thinking halfway rationally of what she had done, instinct told her that she could never have summoned the courage to pull the trigger of Buck's gun. Something Tenn had said, something about the nightmare she would live if she ever discovered she had been wrong about him, had sharply penetrated the barrier of her emotions and prodded her sanity to assert itself.

She knew now with absolute certainty that she could never have shot Tenn. She could still feel the weight of the blanket dropping onto her hand to release the trigger without her mind willing it, could still smell that acrid stench of powder-burned wool as Tenn's arm had held her those brief seconds while he shot the lock off the inner door.

Just now as she recalled how powerful, yet gentle, the grip of his arm had been, she saw a small figure approaching out of the downstreet shadows beyond the last lighted store window. And in sudden panic over the chance that this might be someone she knew, she slowed her stride and considered crossing the street.

The next moment she recognized Mary Stone and, because they were friends, knew she couldn't avoid the girl this openly. So she walked straight on, trying to calm herself so as not to betray how overwrought she was.

But she shortly discovered she had failed in this. For Mary's welcoming smile quickly faded as they met, her eyes showing a troubled look. "What's wrong, Sheila? Has something happened?"

Mary's concern and the gentleness of her tone affected Sheila strangely, making her think that here was exactly what she had been needing, the reassuring presence of someone she trusted and could confide in. And in real thankfulness at no longer being alone with her torment, she took Mary's arm, saying in a voice that quavered, "Please walk home with me. Something has . . . I've just done something really dreadful."

Mary's look of concern deepened. "Your mother and I heard shooting up here. I've just left her. Was it . . . has it something to do with that?"

"I'm afraid so." Sheila tried to steady her voice, couldn't. "I . . . I'd gone to the jail to see Tenn. I'd taken Buck's gun with me. Then —"

"A gun?" Mary halted sharply. "Why?"

Sheila closed her eyes a moment. "Because I was out of my mind, I suppose. But I went there to use it on Bill Tenn."

"Oh, no," Mary cried, so softly the words were barely audible. "You shot him?"

"I didn't. I couldn't go through with it. He took the gun away from me and broke jail, got away."

Sheila couldn't understand the outright delight that rid Mary's hazel eyes of their shocked look. "You're glad?" she asked wonderingly.

"Yes. Of course I'm . . ." Mary checked her words, realizing how they must sound to anyone who had every reason for despising Tenn. She went on lamely, "That is, I . . . what if you found out later you'd been wrong about him?"

"You're saying the same thing he did." Sheila studied her friend a moment. "You don't think he killed Buck?"

Mary's cheeks took on color. "I didn't say that."

"But you think it."

"All right, yes, I do think it."

Sheila was bewildered. "How can you when the whole town thinks differently?"

"Don't ask me why, Sheila. I haven't the right to tell you."

Sheila sensed that something important backed this girl's stubborn words. "Mary, Buck is dead. If you know something I don't, haven't I the right to know what it is?"

For a moment Mary was undecided. But then she knew without question what both her father and John Updyke would do in her place just now. "You do have the right," she answered gravely. "They'll simply have to understand my telling you."

"Who will?"

"Dad and John Updyke."

"What have they to do with all this?"

Mary began explaining, telling Sheila what she had told John Updyke less than half an hour ago. She left nothing unsaid, and as they walked steadily on, approaching the lights of the Flynn house, she once interrupted herself to say, "They were standing almost here, where we are now."

Her voice had gone silent by the time they came in on the yard gate and the shovelled path banked high with snow. And when Sheila didn't say anything, Mary told her, "This could mean absolutely nothing."

"Yet it could mean a lot." Sheila ran the back of a hand across her forehead in a gesture eloquent of her bewilderment. "It's almost too much to take in. Sam hasn't mentioned their quarreling. I even think I remember . . ."

When she didn't continue, Mary asked, "Remember what?"

"Nothing. It may come to me later."

Sheila knew it would never come to her more forcefully, more completely, than she was remembering it now. For it was almost as though Sam Akers was here beside her rather than Mary, saying as he had the morning after Buck had been killed, the morning of the funeral. *If I'd only been anywhere around when it happened, they'd be burying Tenn along with Buck this morning.*

Sam Akers had nicely timed his arrival at the muck dump below the drain tunnel outlet this evening. He had eaten his supper early and tied his horse in the brush below while there was still enough light left to see to make the climb. The going was rough and the drifts were deep along this slope that lay barely three hundred yards south of the joining of Cedar Street and the foot of the pass road.

He took his time, carrying a lantern and a long roll of drafting paper, pausing now and then to catch his breath. He didn't particularly care if he was seen up here, there being half a dozen reasons he could give for this after-hours visit to the branch tunnel. Yet he was hoping he wouldn't be seen, and as he finally climbed up across the dump and stooped to enter the drain tunnel he was fairly sure he hadn't been.

To play it doubly safe, he trudged a dozen steps into the dark hole before pausing to remove his heavy coat and light the lantern. When the wick had caught he levered down the chimney and forgot himself, straightening and banging his head hard against the low ceiling. But he was in good spirits tonight and, after grunting a solemn oath, chuckled at recollection of how the crews had complained on being assigned to work this particular job. Because of the cramped dimensions of the tunnel and the wetness underfoot, the men had worked shorter shifts and demanded higher pay, which he had grudgingly given them.

Bent over, his boots sloshing through inch-deep flowing water, he walked steadily on toward the main tunnel, thus putting himself well out of hearing of the two gunshots that sounded from the center of town some ten mintues later.

He had walked this so many times that, just to test himself, he trudged on looking almost straight down, counting three hundred and seventy-nine steps before glancing ahead. There, sure enough, was the shored-in door closing off the steep side shaft following the vein Buck Flynn had had the good fortune to stumble onto.

"Not so good for him." Akers spoke aloud as he reached out, took the peg from the hasp and pulled the door open.

Once through the door he pulled it shut and began the climb. For perhaps fifty feet the mucking crews had channeled steps in the granite. Further on was a ladder that climbed gently at first, then more steeply to a ledge. From that point on another series of ladders angled sharply off to the right.

The wandering plan of this pretended air-shaft had at first worried Akers. The vein hadn't been at all accommodating, hadn't followed an orderly, straight-up line as should a true air-shaft. Yet he had thought out an explanation for this, should anyone — particularly Ralph Burgess — ever inquire as to the meanderings of the hole. Soft rock, would be Akers' explanation. He had made the hole as cheaply as he could, hoping to clear out some of the damp, dead air that had made the digging of the drain tunnel so difficult. And if Burgess should ever investigate and ask why the shaft hadn't been finished, Akers would tell him the simple truth. Once the drain outlet was finished the air had freshened and the shaft was no longer needed.

His reason for being here tonight was to compare this plan Buck had drawn something like a month ago with the actual layout of the glory hole they had worked so recently. And now as he reached the end of the topmost ladder and moved well away from it, Akers set the lantern down, unrolled Buck's drawing and anchored its corners with pieces of rock. Then, taking a six-foot wooden rule from the pocket of his coat, he picked up the lantern and began making his measurements.

This chore, plus lightly sketching in the most recent excavations, took him all of thirty minutes. His final act was to climb a section of rickety scaffolding and, on its topmost platform, hold the lantern high in an attempt to estimate the distance to the rough granite ceiling of the hole high overhead. Twenty more feet, he decided.

When he had finally finished and was studying the elevation, then the plan sketch, a frown of annoyance slowly settled across Akers' heavy features. According to the sketches, Buck had estimated that the vein continued diagonally upward from a point above already cleared away. In one lower corner of the sheet was a crudely drawn layout for shoring in the big hole.

His annoyance was occasioned by the prospect of having to bring heavy timbers in here to brace against the ceiling so as to avoid a cave-in and protect his crews as they worked higher along the vein. The expense of the shoring was something he disliked. Yet he was resigned to it finally as he pocketed the rule, rolled up the plan and started back down the ladder, troubled only by the thought that he would be running some risk in bringing a timber crew, not Chinamen, into this big hole.

But by the time he reached the tunnel below, his scheming mind had thought of something. There were two Chinamen and a newly-hired emigrant Swede working as helpers with the timber crew in the main tunnel. They, with his own help if need be, would do the shoring.

On the way out of the tunnel he began thinking again of his shortage of teams. With Bill Tenn in jail, he saw it as impossible that Burgess would go ahead with his plan for bringing the Moguls over the pass. And by the time he had reached the end of the tunnel and blown out the lantern, he had decided to ride on out to the horse camp and begin dickering through the old man for the purchase of Tenn's animals.

It was dark now, and as he carefully waded the drifts down along the steep face of the muck dump he experienced an exultant moment in thinking that, two feet below the soles of his boots, lay ton upon ton of rich silver-bearing ore. It would remain hidden here until he had finished work on the main tunnel. After that he would unobtrusively file his claim on that section of the mountain below which the vein ran, and buy this patch of ground where the muck dump lay.

He was in high spirits some ten mintues later as he rode in on Tenn's camp. His one encounter with Tenn's helper had shown him that the old man was salty, that he would be unfriendly. That didn't matter. What did matter was the teams.

As his horse came in on the fire, Early Jordan's shape suddenly rose from behind the lean-to. The old man shaded his eyes against the fire's light, looking toward Akers and calling, "Any luck?"

"Luck?" Akers echoed, closing in and finally drawing rein.

"Oh, it's you." Jordan's tone was dry-edged, hostile. "Thought it was one of the posse come back for a look-see."

"Posse?" Akers could make no sense of the word.

"Posse's what I said," the other bridled. Then, evidently deciding that Akers' bewilderment was genuine, he asked, "You haven't heard?"

"What should I have heard?"

"Something that'll tickle your funny bone, yours especially." Early Jordan smiled broadly. "Bill's busted jail. Flown the coop. Lit out for yonder, free as the breeze."

Akers sat stunned, speechless, whereupon the old man eyed him with a scowl. "So you didn't know, eh? Then why are you here? Well, I got me a notion. You're here because, thinks you, with poor Bill locked up you'll just be the soul of generosity and take these teams off his hands, so long as he hasn't any need for them. Not at a fair price, understand. But what does a man in the jail for life care about a fair price? He'd sell for 'most anything. Was that what you had in mind?"

"Better button your lip, old man." Akers' tone was mild, for he was too absorbed in thinking of Tenn's escape to resent what had been said.

"Button my lip, eh?" Early Jordan's right hand that had so far been out of sight behind the canvas suddenly lifted to lay a Winchester across the lean-to's top pole.

"Button my lip, my eye. You're the slippery sidewinder that brought all this trouble on in the first place, tryin' to rob Bill blind. Well, mister, you've got a surprise coming, a big one."

The outright contempt larding the words was something Sam Akers would never have tolerated had he not been staring at the dully gleaming barrel of the rifle. It meant he had to sit here and take this from the old hellion, though just now he saw it as being beneath him to say anything.

"Yes, sir, a mighty fine surprise," Early shortly told him. "Come sunup tomorrow and these teams of Bill's head out over the mountain. To drag a pair of engines that'll cost you dear. Y' hear, we're making that haul for the railroad after all."

"You? You're going to do it?"

Akers was laughing as Jordan came back at him, "Who else but me?"

"It'll be fun watching you try. Tenn might've turned the trick, but not you."

"Brother, you got a jim dandy of a jolt coming." Akers couldn't guess what lay behind the old man's look of smugness then as Jordan added, "Wait and see. But for right now you can take that sway-back nag out of here. With your hands right like they are, restin' real easy on the horn."

Akers nodded almost pleasantly, pulling rein and turning away from the lean-to. He tried to think of something to say in parting that would put the old man in his place, but couldn't. Yet in another moment he hardly cared as he kicked his animal's flanks and jogged away in the darkness toward the head of the street.

Five minutes later he was passing the *Buena Vista* and seeing something he hadn't thought he would, a light shining from the side window of the marshal's office. A horse stood at the the rail in front of the shoe shop. And in considerable surprise at the possibility of Bushrod being in town, he tied his grey alongside the other animal and took the stairway to the jail two steps at a time.

Red Bushrod was alone in the office and glanced up in annoyance at the sound of the door opening. But when he saw who it was he tilted back in the chair behind the rickety table that served him as a desk. He stretched out and yawned, saying, " 'Evening, Akers. You're a little late for the excitement."

"So I hear. This is a hell of a note, your letting that lanky devil get away." A disarming smile tempering his words, Akers sauntered across and looked down to see a map spread on the table. Nodding to it, he asked, "Don't you know this country well enough not to need that?"

"You'd think so. But it helps jog a man's memory. There's got to be some sort of system on how we go about looking for Tenn come morning."

"Thought you'd be out trying that right now."

"I was for a time. For long enough to get my men placed. But we can't do much in the dark." Bushrod thought back on what old Jordan had said earlier. Now he saw the humor of it and chuckled dryly. "Ever try tracking in the dark?"

"Not me. That's out of my line."

The law man reached over and swept a hand across the map. "A lot of country off here. It'd take twenty men maybe a month to look into every cut and draw." Very respectfully, he looked up to ask, "You got any ideas on how to go about this?"

"Not a one. I'd guess your man's gone for good."

"That's my guess, too. And it looks like more snow before morning, which won't help none."

"What do you know so far?"

"About Tenn?" Bushrod shrugged. "Don't know much, but I can suspect a lot. First off, on the way back here I picked up a horse he'd stole. Which means he probably got to his camp, put his saddle on the best nag in his string and took out with grub and blankets and a rifle. With the head start he'll have by morning, we shouldn't stand a prayer of ever catching him."

"Think he's headed out of the country then?"

"Why wouldn't he be, hot as it is here for him?"

A thought struck Akers then. "What'll happen to these teams he brought in?"

The marshal lifted his hands from the desk, let them fall. "Who's to know? He's probably told Jordan either to sell or drive 'em back home."

"What about his hauling those engines over here for Burgess?"

Bushrod shrugged. "His chances for that are long gone."

"Are they? Couldn't the old man go ahead with it?"

"Him? A busted down old cow nurse take on a chore like that? Hunh-uh. And why would he want to?"

"Just thought he might is all."

They talked a little longer before Akers made his exit. He went down the stairway slowly, absorbed in trying to see through the enigma of Early Jordan's intentions. And his preoccupation remained unbroken as he led his horse across to the livery and turned the animal over to the hostler.

Pacing slowly back up the street, heading for the hotel, he was trying to see Jordan's plan for taking the teams to Granite as logical. Yet he couldn't. It was illogical, pointless, unless . . . *Unless he's doing it for Tenn. Or better, with him.*

The thought came suddenly with such force that it drew him to a halt. As he stood there feeling the crisp chill riding the night air, his hand fumbled inside his coat for a cheroot. He bit the end from it, struck his match on an awning post and waned slowly on, beginning to see more clearly certain things that had puzzled him until now.

First, as Bushrod had said, Jordan wasn't the man to tackle the job of hauling the Moguls over the pass completely on his own. He doubted that Burgess would even consider letting the old man make a try. Yet Jordan had seemed to know something, had given him that half-smiling look when he insisted that the engines were to come across.

Had Ralph Burgess in these past four days since Tenn's arrest found another man he felt was responsible to boss the job? Akers doubted it. Then it naturally followed that old Jordan had some special knowledge of how it could be done.

His hunch of a minute ago appeared sound now. As Bushrod had said, there was a lot of country up in the hills a man could hide in. What, then, was to stop Tenn from hiding out near Granite and seeing Jordan often enough to supervise the building of the sleds, even the actual hauling of the engines? And wouldn't Burgess, wanting the Moguls on the Pinetop workings as badly as he must want them, close an eye to the letter of the law and ask no questions so long as he got what he was after?

Akers was certain now that he had discovered what lay behind Jordan's smug assertion of a quarter hour ago. And his thinking leaped ahead to tomorrow and the following days. The Moguls weren't coming over the pass if he had his way.

He went into the *Buena Vista*'s lobby hoping he could go straight up to his room and think this thing through, plan what he had to do. He was taking his room key from the man at the desk when he heard someone coming in behind him. "Too bad about Sheila, Sam."

Akers turned to find Harvey Ford standing there. "What about Sheila?"

"You hadn't heard?" Ford was amazed.

"Why, it was because of her Tenn got away. Bushrod thinks she took a gun in to him."

That was the beginning of a long argument that rid Sam Akers' mind of everything but the immediate worry of wondering just how much of the rumor Ford was repeating could be true.

John Updyke rode in on Early Jordan's breakfast fire in a light fall of snow at half past six the next morning before it had even begun to get light.

His appearance seemed incongruous to Jordan, who had never seen him wearing anything but his rough grey suit. This morning Updyke's thinness was relieved by a thick shortcoat covering two wool shirts and a heavy sweater. The lawyer's wide hat was worn, sweat-stained, and the toes of his scuffed boots turned up to betray long acquaintance with the stirrup.

Early was impressed, sensing that this outfit belonged to no tenderfoot. So his invitation, "Light and put some of this hot stuff into you before we get going, lawyer," was genuine, hearty.

Updyke swung down off the back of the bay horse, looping reins over the lean-to's nearest front pole. He pulled off his mittens and accepted the pie-tin and the cup of coffee

Early offered him with a, "Look now, I've already eaten," eyeing the rich stew filling the plate.

"You're still a growing man. And we've got a day's work ahead of us. Put it in you."

John Updyke hunkered down on his heels and emptied the plate in silence, another thing that added to the healthy respect in which Early Jordan was beginning to hold him. For the old man, knowing that this friend of Bill's was going into this blind, had expected to have to spend the first quarter-hour answering a lot of questions.

Finally, as a wan grey light was beginning to reveal the snowy sweep of this upper end of the valley, Early picked up the graniteware coffee pot and offered it. "Another touch before I throw it on the fire?"

Updyke nodded and Early filled his cup. When the lawyer still had no questions, Early could no longer resist asking, "You're not the least mite curious?"

John Updyke knew his man well enough to shrug and say, "Who wouldn't be? But you'll tell me what it's all about when the proper time comes."

"That time's now." Early paused momentarily, thinking out how he should say it. Then: "It's like this. Last night when Bill was gatherin' his possibles and getting ready to scoot out of here, he says, 'Early, we're going to need help. And the one man I'd trust to help is John Updyke.' Which to me means Bill thinks you're all wool and two yards wide."

"Glad he's counting me in on whatever you're up to."

"Well, sir, we aim to do plenty. With your help. First —"

" 'We'?" Updyke interrupted sharply.

"Sure. Me and Bill. I'm to take these teams across, you're to get things set with Burgess. Then Bill will —"

"You mean he's not getting out of the country?"

Early Jordan shook his head. "Not that one. He's stayin', hiding out in the brush and hoping to get to me now and then to tell me how to make this haul."

Updyke shook his head in bafflement, his expression sober, worried. "Suppose they find him and bring him in? Even if he's brought in alive I'd have the devil of a time filing an appeal on the trial after this."

"He'll be all right." Jordan brushed away a big flake of snow that had settled on his nose. "He's a chip square off the old block. Why, I've known his father, Frank, to —"

"Let's stick to Bill," the lawyer cut in. "Why's he so set on going through with this when it may mean his neck?"

"Why? Honesty's why. Honesty and debt. When old Frank went under, what he owed others nearly dragged them down with him. Bill wouldn't stand for that and took on every dollar the old man owed. Since then, five years back, there's been many a time when he didn't know who'd stake him to his next sack of grub. He's earned plenty but he's turned it all over to others."

"His father was travelling on a shoestring?"

"That he wasn't." Jordan went on talking, his look bleak as he told of those grim months five years ago when Texas fever had ravaged Frank Tenn's range. And presently he was saying, "The other night Bill told me he'd be in the clear in one more year, running his own brand again. Losing that sale to Akers lost him his chance. But then this contract he's signed with that railroad man brightens his prospects considerable."

He eyed Updyke half-angrily then to ask, "Now you understand why you and me got to pitch in and bring this off? Because if you don't, mister, you can clear on out and I'll chouse this horseflesh across that pass on my own."

"I understand, Early." Updyke tossed the coffee grounds from his cup into the snow and, rising, said, "Let's get at it."

Some five minutes later neither of them saw Sam Akers through the curtain of gently falling snow, or heard the deadened hoof falls of his animal as he passed the camp on his way to his office earlier than usual, wanting to clean up a few urgent matters so he could later get away to call on Sheila.

He might have done just that if he hadn't recognized John Updyke as the man helping old Jordan load the pack-mare. And as he went on, his curiosity mounting, he was revising his plans for the day.

Akers spent only two minutes in his office, reappearing with a scabbarded rifle under his arm. When he shortly rode back toward town he swung wide of the horse camp, not seeing Updyke and Jordan as they pulled away the brush closing in the pocket where the teams had been held.

Sam Akers was playing a hunch, one he supposed had but a remote chance of paying off. But he often played these hunches and he was occasionally very, very lucky.

That hunch presently took him out Pine-top's Cedar Street and up the pass road.

This early morning Bill Tenn pushed the sorrel steadily on across the broken country below the pass, oocasionally getting his bearings as the misty fall of snow would thin and momentarily let him glimpse some recognizable peak or ridge in the near distance. It was bitter cold and he would now and then get down and plod through the deep snow so as to warm himself and save the sorrel.

As the first hour passed he was absorbed in thinking of last night, in wondering now if he had had the right to involve Early Jordan, and perhaps John Updyke, so deeply in his affairs. But most of all he was thinking of Sheila Flynn.

Last night, after he had circled the fires of the tunnel camp and then struck west into the timbered hills, his thoughts of Buck Flynn's sister had so engrossed him that they had nearly outweighed the urgency of putting distance between him and Pinetop. Toward midnight, after he had climbed perhaps five miles into the foothills, he made a cold camp along a shallow draw, throwing his blankets under a ledge only to lie awake another hour trying to recall each detail of those minutes in the jail with Sheila.

He had still been able to feel the impact of her loveliness, and of the loathing and contempt for him that had brightened her green eyes. And when he finally fell asleep he had been troubled more by the knowledge of her despising him than by any worry over the chance of someone stumbling upon his hiding place before morning.

Just now as her image came before his mind's eye again he told himself, *John just might rig it so I can see her*. And the thought made him push on faster.

In another hour he was high along a pine slope flanking the pass, looking down on the road, obscured by the haze of falling snow. He came aground and, standing with hand on the sorrel's nose, carefully studied the sweep of ground below.

It was long minutes before the snow thinned enough to let him see the road, and the gleam of a fire against the greyness along a low ridge several hundred yards above it. He went to the saddle once more and worked down closer to the blaze, and presently, from a greater height, saw two men standing in the fire's wan light.

These would be men Red Bushrod had put up here to be on the lookout for him. Convinced of that, he crossed to the back side of the ridge and rode down-country, presently circling to bring himself in sight of the road again some two miles below. Once more he came aground and spent long minutes studying the hazed and winding stretch of road and the further slopes.

It was while he stood there that he saw a lone rider climbing toward the pass. And as the man drew near, his massive bulk was unmistakably recognizable. Bill spent a few moments wondering what was bringing Sam Akers over the pass today, deciding finally that the man must have business with the railroad across in Granite. The thought of Akers being so close to him brought a smile to his lean face. For he had long ago understood the importance Akers must attach to the chance of Burgess's engines working the Pinetop tunnel, and now it pleased him to imagine what the big man's reaction was to be once he discovered that the plan had not been abandoned.

Minutes later, as he lost sight of Akers and began a second swing downward, this time trying to keep the road in sight, he was feeling a stir of anticipation in thinking that Early and his teams couldn't be far below. For last night the old man had agreed to break camp and put the teams on the road at daybreak. He had also offered to go into town, find John Updyke and ask him to get the word to Ralph Burgess that they were going ahead with the contract for hauling the Moguls.

When he did see the long string of animals he didn't at first recognize them, instead taking them for a bare high bank flanking the far side of the road. Then, when that dark line moved, he knew it for what it was and headed down there, a hard excitement stirring in him.

Closer in, he saw the old man riding at the head of the string alongside the bell mare. But what laid a delighted smile across his face was the sight of John Updyke, barely recognizable through the curtain of snow, riding the drag.

He angled across toward the tail of the column, shortly putting the sorrel down through a dense growth of oak brush bordering the road. Updyke heard the horse and looked around in startlement. And as Bill came in alongside him his face was slack with surprise.

"You damned Indian. You shouldn't be here."

But then the lawyer was smiling warmly as Bill told him, "It was too good a chance to miss."

"You're asking for trouble. Bushrod's got men up above."

Bill nodded. "A pair. I've just come from looking them over. And from seeing Akers on his way across."

"Akers? Where?"

"He went past maybe fifteen minutes ago. Probably on his way to see Burgess."

"Speaking of Burgess, I'll see him today and try and get him to let us go ahead with the contract."

"You will on one condition, John." Bill gave

the lawyer a serious glance. "He's to rewrite the contract. In both our names, yours and mine."

"Mine?" Updyke was incredulous. "Why, in the name of —"

"Because you're someone he trusts. Because Early and I couldn't go ahead on this without your help."

Updyke shook his head. Then, with a half-smiling look, he said, "You let Early and me figure out that end of it. Now where'll you be in case we want to find you?"

"Been thinking about that. Pace's old logging camp up there on Baldy seems the likeliest —"

The air whip of a bullet laid a small sound against the stillness, followed a split second later by the brittle *crack!* of a rifle sounding from above.

Bill reined the sorrel hard aside, his glance whipping ahead along the strung-out column of mares and geldings. He saw Sam Akers running a horse hard toward him along the column, plainly saw the man levering another shell into the chamber of a rifle as he raised it to shoulder.

He whipped his coat aside and drew Buck Flynn's Colt's from holster. He swung the sorrel sharply around, aimed the gun skyward and thumbed off two quick-timed shots.

Those thundering blasts made the animals directly ahead jump, then bolt. And as they spread out in panic, blocking the road, Bill raked the sorrel's flanks with spur and started away at a hard run.

IV

The sorrel had lunged fifty yards along the snowy road when Bill felt the animal break stride momentarily, then go smoothly on as Akers' rifle exploded behind him a second time.

He reined sharply to one side, a hurried glance back there showing him John Updyke's high shape, and Akers' taller one, outlined above the backs of the mares and geldings jamming the road. And now with the sorrel carrying him into the head of a bend and a high bank suddenly blocking his view of the upper road, he sensed that Akers was in the clear and riding fast toward him.

He leaned back on the reins and reached for the Winchester in the scabbard under his leg. He was vaulting from the saddle before the sorrel had quite stopped. Dropping rein, he went to a knee and levelled the rifle at the exact instant Akers' animal pounded into sight beyond the bank's edge barely a hundred feet away.

There was a split-second when he was looking at Sam Akers' wide chest across his sights.

He checked himself, dropped to a broader target and squeezed trigger. The sharp pound of the rifle seemed to loosen every muscle in the animal Akers rode. Its forelegs buckled, it went down sideward in a diving, cartwheeling sprawl. Akers was thrown clear, and as he hit the rutted snow with a shoulder and rolled over and over the rifle flew from his grasp.

Bill had a second's clear sight of the wounded horse skidding in a spray of flying snow toward Akers before he wheeled, swung into the saddle and sawed the sorrel hard away and off the road, up through the drifts toward a fringe of pines close ahead along the face of a ridge to the south. He used the spur savagely, his long frame tight against the expected slam of a bullet. Yet as the horse made those final lunges that took him into the trees no sound came from below.

When he was well into the pines, Bill slowed the sorrel and looked around and down. The light fog of falling snow let him see big Sam Akers only now getting awkwardly to his feet and moving clear of his animal's flailing hooves. He plainly saw the man reach under coat, draw a pistol and fire a shot that put his mount out of its misery.

But when Akers lifted the gun over his head then and fired three quick-timed shots that boomed hollowly up along the slope, Bill's momentary feeling of relief died with the knowledge that this must be a signal to the men Bushrod had put above to watch the pass. And as he rode deeper into the timber, still climbing, he knew he had probably only a quarter-hour's head start on the possemen.

He remembered the sorrel's break in stride back there on the road now and, though the animal didn't appear to be hurt, he reined in and came aground again to discover a deep, bleeding gouge along the right side of the horse's rump. With that stark evidence of how close Akers' last shot had come to deciding this, he set about stopping the flow of blood, holding handfuls of snow over the wound.

The red-stained snow he tossed aside would be an encouraging sign when Bushrod's men presently tracked him to this point. Following him through this deep snow would be a simple matter in the beginning and far simpler as the day wore on and the sorrel tired from loss of blood. Even though the darkening sky gave promise of a heavier fall of snow, they would be too close behind him to let him hope that his tracks would be covered over. And a strong urgency was driving him when he presently went on, soon topping the ridge to look off across the snow-hazed hills stretching south-ward.

How to confound Akers and the others to gain time he would badly need later today was something he was trying to think out now as he looked into the southeast toward the faintly discernable shadow of a lower ridge he supposed must be nearly a mile distant. The slope immediately below was fairly steep and rocky, swept clean of snow except for what little lay along numerous ledges. Wind and yesterday's light thaw had laid the further stretch bare all the way to its foot where, far downward and to the east, he could make out a patch of grey color that was unmistakably a stand of aspen trees.

Examining the line of that far ridge and its joining with this slope below, even the poor light and the wind-drifting banners of snow let him see that it rose so sheerly no rider would ever think of trying to climb it. Off to his right, westward, the escarpment had the look of being even steeper as it swung to join this near bare ridge face in the upper distance. Beyond, he knew, lay the notch where the road crossed the head of Dead Man.

A man wanting to put distance between him and the road had little choice here except to make a long downward traverse across the thinly whitened rock below, head into the aspens and then up the east end of that far ridge.

Deciding this had taken him but scant seconds, and as he turned his horse on down toward the first stretch of bare rock, trying to ease his weight into the awkward angle of the saddle, he was feeling a let-down from the tension of five minutes ago. The creak of leather, the rhythmic ring of the sorrel's shoes striking rock, and presently a false sense of security that came when the snow thickened, all threatened to dull his wariness. He had to keep forcing himself to stay alert, for this was slow, tricky going he supposed might last for the next twenty minutes.

Twenty minutes. He was suddenly jolted by a thought, and told himself, *You could use it,* tightening rein so that the sorrel came to a stand. Then he was trying to put himself in the place of Bushrod's two men — or three, if they could persuade Early Jordan to loan Akers a mount — who would presently be riding from above following the line of his tracks as they swung eastward and down into the bare stretch.

They, as he had, would see that the only way off this ridge and away from the road lay to the southeast toward the aspens below. With his tracks pointing directly that way, they would drop along this ridge face and at its base cast around until they came across his sign again, a relatively easy chore.

And if they don't find tracks then it's those

twenty minutes wasted. Along with maybe thirty more climbing back.

He felt a faint excitement run through him as, turning and putting his weight in one stirrup, he looked upward toward the pass. This bare slope ran on for better than a mile before it became obscured by the snow fog. If he rode even that distance he would be well beyond the point where he had topped the ridge, would be over the hump from the road and travelling almost parallel to it. And if he rode further, two miles perhaps, he would be within sight of the road at the top of the pass again.

If the two men he had earlier seen up there hadn't heard Akers' shots, if they were still watching the road and the reach of hills to either side, he ran no small risk in riding that way, for this steady fall of snow might thin or even die away at any moment.

But if Sam Akers' shots had taken effect the pass was clear.

Bill Tenn had taken many chances over the past five years, few of which had been foolish. But some had involved a measure of risk. Some hadn't proved out, most had. This one might.

Because his life had lately become something of a gamble at best, and because the difficult years had nurtured in him a streak of fatalism that had taught him to shrug off fear as a thing that only harmed a man, he turned back now. He drew the Winchester from its boot and laid it across the saddle, his wary glance roving the misty upper slope as he headed for Dead Man.

That night Early Jordan was squatting alongside his supper fire near the rail fence of a pasture a mile to the north of Granite when a rider came in out of the snow-swirling blackness and pulled his grey horse to a stand well within the light.

This was the fifth time this man the sheriff had put out here to watch the camp had circled the pasture and come past the fire. And now Jordan laid aside a skillet he had been scouring with snow, dryly asking, "What, you haven't caught him yet?"

"Lay off, will you?"

The speaker, a small man, was red-faced with the cold. Noticing this and weighing the mildness of his tone, Early was prompted to end the feud between them that had lasted the past two hours. "Light and thaw out, friend. Put some of this hot stuff in you."

"No can do." The other wistfully eyed a big graniteware pot sitting alongside the blaze.

"Hell, I wouldn't bite. Your law man didn't say you couldn't keep from turning into a chunk of ice, did he?"

"He said to keep an eye out for your partner in case he sneaks in for grub and a fresh horse. Can I do that loafin' here with you?"

"Then freeze your marrow for all of me."

The rider reined on away from the fire as he had every other time, only this time Early told himself, *One more round and he'll be ready to smoke the pipe.*

As the other's shape faded into the blackness, he tried to forget his worry over Bill by thinking of what a snug pasture Burgess had found for the teams. A barnful of wild timothy lay off there at the near corner, a creek cut through the fence on the side toward the hills. This fire and the lean-to were sheltered from the wind by a stand of pines two hundred yards to the west. It was as nice a . . .

A wad of snow dropped into the fire almost at Jordan's feet, sending up a shower of sparks and hissing so that he jumped back a step. He stared around in puzzlement, then squinted up at the myriad snowflakes drifting out of the blackness.

His glance was swinging down once more when a second ball of snow arced in out of the night and stung him on the leg.

Early swore softly, a hard excitement pounding in him. Just by chance he had seen where that second snowball had come from.

And now, as casually as he could, he left the fire and sauntered on out beyond its light. He had taken only half a dozen more strides when he made out a heavy shadow against the night close ahead.

"Bill?" He was almost afraid of the answer he would get.

"Right here, Early."

A blend of gladness and alarm made the old man's heart pound. He could see Bill plainly now, see him standing alongside the leggy sorrel. And suddenly he felt warm inside and could ignore the fact that his coat lay back there under the lean-to, that nothing but a wool shirt and heavy underwear separated his scrawny upper body from the stinging cold.

He stretched out a hand as he walked in on his friend, breathing almost prayerfully, "Son, you're daft as they come to be here."

"Had a time finding you, Early."

"You're all in one piece?"

"Sure am. But Rusty here isn't."

Bill hadn't seen the old man's outstretched hand, so Early took him by the arm now as though wanting to convince himself he wasn't imagining all this. Then he realized what Bill had just said and quickly asked, "Something wrong?"

"Some of Akers' lead took a chunk off his

hide this morning. He's lost blood and gone stiff. Want to swap him for the claybank, the one I —"

"Sure. But it's all wrong you being this close to camp. Why, not five minutes ago a man the law's put out here —"

"I know. He's off there riding the far side of the fence now."

Early sighed gustily in relief. "Bushrod's asked the sheriff's help in hunting you down, Bill. They've put men out from town to cover all this side of the mountain. Come morning they're going after you for keeps."

"Come morning there'll be half a foot of new snow. By then I'll be long gone from here."

"Now you're talking. Put plenty of miles behind you tonight. Head north, into country you know. I can load you with enough grub to —"

"No, Early. I've got all the grub I need to last me while I hole up in that logging camp on Baldy."

"Good Lord, you're sticking around? Why?"

"To help work out that contract if Burgess will let us go ahead with it. What luck did John have today?"

"We're set with Burgess. But you can't stay around here and risk getting a hole through you. I'll slide those confounded steam en-

144

gines over the mountain. Now use your head and —"

"And how would you go about building a sled for an engine?"

"How?" Jordan set his jaw stubbornly. "Got it all figured. Build a small sled for the little wheels up front, a bigger one for the back."

"Wouldn't work." Bill's tone was gentle, patient. "You'll need a big sled for the engine, a smaller one for the tender. With a rig behind the big one so teams can pull from the back as well as the front. And these sleds should be built a certain way."

"Tell me how and that's the way they'll be rigged. Only you get the devil gone and stay clear of here."

The darkness barely let Jordan make out Bill's shake of the head. "I'm not running, Early. So lay off reading the sermon."

Jordan sensed the iron underlying the mildness in his friend's voice and, knowing further argument was useless, muttered a low oath. Then Bill was telling him, "You'll find the right kind of logs close to the road about two miles up toward the pass from town here. Big spruce logs, tough as they come. Tomorrow get your measurements on the engine and take your crew up there. Cut your runner logs eight to ten feet longer than your load. Axe them flat on the bottom side till the flat part's say a foot and a half wide. Then cut a two-inch groove deep down the middle of the flat part. By the time you've got all that done I'll have seen you and we can go on from there."

"Seen me where?" The old man was incredulous.

"That'll depend. But I'll manage it."

As Bill stepped back now, threw the near stirrup over the saddle and began loosening the cinch, Early's worry made him forget the ultimatum of some moments ago. "Give this up, son. Light a shuck away from here and leave this to me and Updyke. You can't run a chance like this."

"Which reminds me," Bill drawled. "Sooner or later I'm going to see John and find out what he's run onto about the Flynn killing."

"What could he run onto?"

Early saw Bill's head swing sharply around. "He could get a line on who really killed Flynn. Think I'm just riding out and forgetting that?"

Jordan shook his head, shivering now, cold inside as well as out. "You'll wind up in a pine box just as sure as hell's hot."

Bill ignored the words, pulling the saddle and its bedroll along with the booted Winchester from the sorrel's back now, easing them into the snow and then offering the old man the reins. "Better hurry it, Early."

Jordan took the reins without a further word and led the sorrel on away. As he disappeared Bill eased his high frame down into the snow, at first leaning back against the saddle but then sitting straighter as his tiredness made him begin to nod. He knew he should be watching for the man the sheriff had put out here, but all his weariness would let him do was stare toward the fire and try and forget how deep the chill was cutting into him.

The minutes dragged and he told himself to be patient when he judged Jordan had been gone at least fifteen minutes. But then as five more minutes passed he began worrying, wishing now he had gone with Early into the pasture after the claybank.

Suddenly a shape darker than the night moved in soundlessly from his left and in line with the fire, the shape of a small man astride a big horse. The rider was close, barely ten yards distant, and now as Bill came hard alert he could hear the horse breathing and the man humming softly.

Abruptly the man pulled the grey to a stand and sat sharply outlined, staring toward the fire and straightening slightly as though noticing something strange in what he saw. Slowly, carefully, Bill hunched forward onto his knees and drew the rifle from its scabbard.

He barely had it clear of the leather when the rider started in toward the fire.

The sheriff's man rode well into the light before swinging clumsily aground and stepping over to peer into the lean-to. The distance was too great for Bill to be certain, yet he thought he could read the man's puzzled look that moment.

A sound off to his left made him swing the rifle around now. He was on his feet, thumb on the Winchester's hammer, when Early led the claybank in on him, a hand gripping the animal's nose.

"Make it fast!" Early breathed softly, stridently.

Bill heaved the saddle's heavy weight to the animal's back.

Not bothering about the cinch, he threw his rangy frame astride the claybank. At that instant, as he was ramming the rifle into its boot, the horse at the fire whickered loudly.

Early breathed explosively, "Ride, boy!" seeing the man across there wheel and stare obliquely off into the darkness.

Bill took the claybank away at a soundless walk, hunched forward and right hand lying over the animal's nostrils. And as he faded from sight Early glanced toward the fire to see the sheriff's man pulling an ancient Navy Colt's from under his coat as he moved warily toward the grey.

Early hurried toward the fire as fast as he could then, calling, "Put that thing away. It's only me."

He came into the light a few seconds later, and the other saw him and let the gun fall slowly to his side. "Damn, you sure gave me a scare there. Where you been?"

"Having a look at the gate."

"I could've told you it was shut. Had a look at it my last time past. Now if you don't mind, I'd thank you kindly for a cup of that coffee."

John Updyke wasn't the man to postpone a distasteful chore any longer than necessary. Knowing he would sooner or later have to answer to Red Bushrod for having been seen with Tenn up along Dead Man this morning, he had gone straight to the marshal's office when he got back from Granite shortly after five o'clock.

Bushrod hadn't been there, nor was he at the hotel or Ed Pawl's *Keno and Billiard Emporium*, his favorite hangouts. Updyke had finally given up trying to find him when he met him purely by chance in front of the hotel.

"All right, Red. Let's have it," he had said without preliminary. "Tear that strip off my hide."

Bushrod was oddly sober, showing no trace

of anger as he remarked, "There's not one damned thing I can do to you because you can always claim Tenn met you by accident."

"Which happens to be true."

"Sure. Sure it is," the marshal had stated acidly. "But now I got Akers and some others on my neck. Why didn't I have men all the way along the road, they want to know. Why wasn't I up there myself? John, you've got me string-haltered. I could even lose my job."

"Thought you didn't want it anyway. Didn't you say something about a girl called Nancy last night?"

The law man sighed wearily. "So I did. And maybe I'll be going up there soon to work. But meantime I'm in the soup over this."

"Things'll simmer down, Red."

"Not before they come to a boil first. The sheriff's in this thing now. Did you hear about the reward money?"

"No."

"Well, Akers started the ball rollin' about an hour ago by putting up fifty dollars. Some of Buck's other friends have chipped in and now there's around three hundred. It's dead or alive money, too."

All this was sobering news, adding weight to Updyke's worry over Bill. And he had voiced his one remaining hope by saying, "You've got to catch him first, Red."

"So we do. But as for you, there's going to be someone watching you pretty regular from now on. Just in case you try and meet up with Tenn again."

Having made this pronouncement, Bushrod stalked on down the walk. Updyke stood for all of two minutes digesting what he had just heard, until suddenly he had a thought that made him take out his watch and look at it. Seeing that the hour still lacked twenty minutes of being six o'clock, he hurried up the street to the Stone house hoping to have a word with Mary before her father got home from work.

But Fred Stone was already there, ready to sit down with Mary to the evening meal. They wouldn't listen to the lawyer not sharing it with them even though Updyke called attention to the fact that he was wearing the same outfit he had put on this morning for the ride across the pass with Early Jordan. And as he finally went into the kitchen to wash up, he was baffled as to what reason he could give Stone for his call.

The bookkeeper evidently sensed his feeling of awkwardness, for he shortly told him, "Just in case you haven't already guessed it, it was my notion that Mary go see you last night, John. Now what's this we hear about Akers taking a shot at Tenn up Dead Man today?"

The man's straightforwardness put Updyke completely at his ease. He explained what had happened up along the pass and answered their many questions. Stone was obviously delighted over Bill having managed to elude the posse and Akers. And throughout most of the meal their talk was almost light-hearted, at one point even hilarious as Fred Stone went into lengthy detail regarding Mary's difficulties in fitting a certain portly matron across in Granite earlier in the week.

Once they finished the meal Mary refused to let the men help clear the table. She had no sooner left them than Fred Stone was once again his sober self. "She's remembered more about that set-to of Buck's with Akers, John. But it'll baffle you when she tells it."

He heard Mary coming from the kitchen then and turned to her. "Time to come out with it, sis. John's curious."

The smile the girl had given Updyke on entering the room thinned now, died. She took her chair once more, pushed the napkin aside and leaned against the table, arms folded across her breasts and her look grave as she eyed the lawyer. "Can you guess why they'd be talking about silver and claims?"

At John Updyke's look of outright amazement, Stone inserted, "I haven't told him any of it yet."

"Oh." Mary frowned, trying to think of how to begin. "This was why I didn't want to tell you last night, John. Because it seemed so . . . so unbelievable they should have been talking of what they were. I've thought back trying to convince myself I must've imagined it all. But I didn't. I'm sure now."

"Silver?" The lawyer's wondering glance shifted to Stone.

"I warned you it wouldn't make sense."

Mary's next words followed closely on the heel of her father's. "It doesn't. But there it is. And here's more. Just before Buck dropped his voice he called Akers a hog, asked him how much he wanted of . . . of what I couldn't tell. But I did hear Buck mention hauling ore to Granite, silver ore. And he said he was filing a claim."

Stone, taking in the lawyer's continuing look of bewilderment, put in, "It's not so impossible. New as I am in this town, I've heard of old Rankin's prospect. Of how long he worked it thinking he was onto something big before he got so crippled and had to give it up."

"Yes, Fred. But that prospect is twenty miles south of here."

"Suppose it is? If even a trace of silver's been found in one part of these hills, why couldn't it be found somewhere else?"

"No reason at all." Over a moment's pause,

Updyke objected, "But Buck was no miner. He worked long hours. When would he have found the time to prospect?"

"That's what stumps Mary and me."

Mary, seeing the doubt that lingered in the lawyer's eyes, insisted, "I can't be wrong about this. And I can't be wrong about Buck being awfully, awfully mad."

Stone shifted in his chair, folding his hands on the cloth and staring down at them. "You're to think about this, John, as I will. But let's forget it for a moment. There's something else I want to say. About why I sent Mary to you."

His glance abruptly lifted, and there was a bleak look in his eyes now. "It may have seemed strange to you, doing as I did when I work for Sam Akers. So I want you to know why I did."

His seriousness was embarrassing to Updyke, who sensed that the man was about to speak of something very personal. And now he quietly stated, "No need to go into the whys and wherefores. The main thing is I appreciate what you two have done. Bill will appreciate it even more."

"I know. But this is something I must get said. You may or may not know Sam Akers, know the kind of man he is. Yet it's important to me that you should know I have to work

154

for him. *Have* to. That's as far as I need go."

Taking in the uneasiness of the lawyer's expression, Stone smiled faintly and came up out of his chair. "Now that that's off my chest, suppose we treat ourselves to something I've been saving for an occasion. Sis, where did I hide it?"

There was a tenderness in the look Mary gave him. "You could begin by looking in mother's trunk in the attic."

"Then you'll excuse me."

Updyke and the girl watched Fred Stone leave the room, and as his deliberate steps sounded up along the carpeted stairway Mary said softly, "He likes you, John. What he's after is a bottle of brandy. Fine brandy. It's a bottle he and mother toasted each other with at their wedding. They . . . dad used to bring it out each year for their anniversary dinner. It's almost empty now and I don't think he's opened it since mother died."

She took in the lawyer's polite yet faintly uncomfortable look. "He would never say more than he did just now about Sam Akers. And he's wrong in a way. Because he doesn't really have to work for the man. It's a debt of honor with him."

Over a slight pause, she went on, "You see, three years ago when Akers bought out the business dad was working for, he seemed a different man. Not so . . . what do I want to say, ambitious?"

"Akers is all of that. And more."

"He's a lot of things we've learned not to like too much. Anyway, mother was quite sick that year and it was important to dad to keep his job. So he stayed on with Akers. Then mother died. She'd been ailing for two years, with doctor after doctor. Dad had borrowed heavily. After it was over Akers offered us the money to settle everything, nearly a thousand dollars. Dad signed a note and has been paying it off out of his salary. It's . . . we'll be in the clear in about six more months."

John Updyke's voice bore a gentle quality as he said, "From what you say you must be helping."

Mary nodded. "Wouldn't you if you wanted to see him get this over with and go on to something better? He isn't paid much, probably because Akers knows he won't leave him owing him so much as a dollar."

They could hear Fred Stone coming back down the stairs now, and she hurried to say quietly, "He wouldn't like it if he knew I'd told you this. But I . . . I wanted you to understand. There's no one finer. He's better than . . ."

When she hesitated, at loss for words, John Updyke reached out and laid a hand on hers, saying nothing, his gesture nevertheless bringing a warm, grateful smile to her eyes.

It was while John Updyke was thanking the Stones for having let him share their evening meal that Sam Akers came out of the *Buena Vista*'s bar and started across the dingy lobby, headed for his second floor room.

He was trying not to limp, and because his left shoulder ached and was badly bruised, hurting each time he moved his arm, he had thrust that hand in the pocket of his coat. He wasn't eating supper, had no appetite at all for food. Even the four whiskies he had taken at the bar hadn't done much to ease the aches and pains brought on by his hard fall from the back of his dying horse up there along the pass road this morning. And the whiskey hadn't thinned his sourness over realizing that he was in no shape to call on Sheila and get the story of her visit to Tenn in the jail last night.

As he came in on the stairway, a man rose from a horse-hair couch alongside the newel post, laid a paper he had been reading on a nearby table and said, "Could I have a minute of your time, Mr. Akers?"

Startled, Akers halted, eyeing the speaker and vaguely remembering having seen him somewhere before. Because he was in no mood for idle conversation, he snapped, "Just about a minute. What is it?"

The other glanced to the clerk behind the counter on the far side of the stairs, lowering his voice to say, "Maybe we ought to step over here."

He turned toward the empty back corner of the lobby. And Akers, following, was all at once interested. Yet his tone didn't betray that interest as the stranger shortly turned to face him once more. "If you're looking for work, see me in the morning at my office."

"But I'm not looking for work." The man smiled faintly. "I'm looking for money."

Sam Akers' eyes mirrored a strong annoyance. "So are a lot of people. What's your name?"

"The name doesn't matter. What does is that I have a way of knowing what goes on in Ralph Burgess's office. Today something happened over there that should be worth fifty dollars to you to know about."

The big man's expression lost its bridling quality. "What?"

Nodding toward the table by the stairway, the other said, "There's a paper lying on that table over there. I'm told you generally carry a sizeable amount of money with you. Suppose you put the fifty inside the paper first of all."

Sam Akers eyed the man coolly a moment

before reaching inside his coat for his wallet. He thumbed some bills from it and stepped across to the table. Sauntering back again, he said crisply, "The fifty's there. If what you're about to tell me is worth it, the paper's yours. If it isn't, I take it up to my room and read it. Now get it said."

"Would the name John Updyke mean anything to you?" At Akers' wary nod, the stranger went on, "I have heard that he paid a call on Burgess today. A call that resulted in Burgess deciding to go ahead with hauling those engines over the pass."

"Who'll make the haul?"

"The old man who's working for Tenn."

"Ralph Burgess's head is full of sawdust." Akers was plainly disturbed over what he had just heard.

"Perhaps it is. But Burgess sent a certain man to the timekeeper after Updyke had gone. Sent him with instructions to pick a crew for the job."

The stranger was seeing a wicked anger in Akers' eyes now as he asked, "Is the money mine?"

"Like hell. I knew all this last night, or most of it. You're giving me nothing for my fifty. I . . ." Pausing, his stare abruptly turning more thoughtful than indignant, Akers asked, "Has Jordan's crew been picked yet?"

"I understand not. He wants eight men who've been both teamsters and loggers. It's a tough combination to find. So far the timekeeper's located only four."

Sam Akers' look underwent a slow change until shortly he was almost smiling. "Suppose I send a good man across, have him there by morning? He's been a teamster, he's worked in a sawmill and a lot of other places."

"Can't help you there."

"You can if you want the fifty."

The stranger's glance shuttled to the table by the stairway. He sighed resignedly. "What's this man's name?"

"Mc . . . McBride."

"Well, I . . ." Shrugging, the stranger gave a spare nod. "If McBride would be at the office at seven sharp in the morning, and if a certain friend of mine happened to be with the timekeeper when he showed up, he might find work."

"Now that's more like it. The money's yours. Only I'll want it back if McBride doesn't get the job."

"If he doesn't, you'll get it back, Mr. Akers."

In less than a minute after Hiram Colter, assistant timekeeper in the C. & W.'s yard offices in Granite, picked up his newspaper and left the lobby, Sam Akers was limping

160

down the street to the livery barn, headed for his tunnel camp.

Seven years of disuse, of mountain rains and winds and heavy snows, had made a near ruin of the logging camp on the broad shoulder of Baldy peak. It sprawled across a wide pocket in a heavy stand of aspen, some of the fallen buildings nearly covered by deep drifts. The blacksmith shed had collapsed two winters ago. Lightning striking a nearby ponderosa had fired the cook shack. The log bunkhouse, sturdiest of all, still stood, although the far end of its roof had caved in.

On his way up through the hills after seeing Early Jordan at the pasture north of Granite last night, Bill had rested an hour deep in a canyon and had cooked a meal over a small fire. Reaching here shortly after midnight, he had thrown his bedroll in the good end of the bunkhouse and tied the claybank inside the canted-over remains of the big sawdust hopper that had served the small sawmill Pace had found it unprofitable to keep in operation.

This morning Bill had slept late, one reason being that he had been bone tired when he rode in, another that the wan grey light of the early day hadn't let him realize how late it was. When he finally left his blankets and stepped to the empty window of the bunkhouse it was to look out and see a thicker smother of snow than yesterday fogging the nearly forgotten vista of this high mountain peak.

It was blistering cold and he was tempted to light a fire. But knowing what he risked in doing that he dismissed the notion and went out to feed the claybank a light measure of grain, afterward saddling the animal and leading him back to the bunkhouse.

He tied his bedroll to the saddle and then used the brim of his hat to whisk the bunkhouse's dirt floor clean of all his tracks. And when he rode down through the trees, eating a cold breakfast of jerky and pan bread, he was wondering how long it would take Bushrod or the sheriff at Granite to send someone up here to look things over.

Though this spot was remote, some ten miles north of Dead Man, he felt certain someone would pass by here eventually. What the outcome of such a visit would be would depend entirely on the sharpness of the caller's eye. For a man knowing how to read sign wouldn't long be deceived by those brushed-over marks in the dust of the bunkhouse floor.

Yet presently the streak of fatalism in him made him shrug aside this worry and decide to deal with it when and if it came along. And as he rode steadily on through the timber his thoughts turned to other things, to the un-looked-for luck of this storm hampering the hunt for him while he moved around in it, and to the good luck of Updyke having convinced Burgess that Early should go ahead with hauling the engines. Finally he was trying to picture just how the sleds should be built.

He was taking a long-odds chance today that would pay off heavily unless he ran into trouble. He thought of it for a time in relation to something he had mentioned to Early last night, his resolve not to leave the country until he had uncovered the truth of how Buck Flynn had died. And it gave him a helpless feeling to know that now, and perhaps for many days to come, his hands were completely tied in even beginning to track down the facts of what had happened that night. He might even never have the chance to uncover them.

In the end he gave up trying to plan on anything as he angled down across canyon and ridge, riding sonthwest. He judged it was getting on toward midday when he swung to the left and, after going steadily on for a good half hour, suddenly came upon the pass road.

He quickly got his bearings on sighting the flat, sheer face of a tall outcrop through the snow-haze almost at the limit of his vision. He was turning away from the road and down in the direction of Granite when all at once the muted jangle of doubletree chains sounded from the road to draw his nerves wire-tight.

Caught in the open, too far from any cover to reach it quickly, he pulled the claybank to a stand and sat stock-still as a three-team hitch ran down the road past him pulling a squat Barlow-Sanderson coach. After it had gone, after he was once again in the trees and the tension was easing away, he felt fairly sure he hadn't been seen. This close call gave him an added sense of luck being with him today. And he went on almost enjoying this game of ghosting through the hills where he knew more than a few men were on the prowl for him.

He had ridden downward for another twenty minutes when distantly, hollowly, the rhythmic strokes of an axe sounded up the pine slope to him. The sound shortly strengthened, was joined by that of a sledge striking an iron wedge. Then in a few more moments came the sudden crackling of breaking branches and the heavy thud of a tree falling to the frozen ground.

He had gone on scarcely another hundred yards before he was looking down through the tall lodgepoles and seeing a silvery-green clump of big spruce and the smoke of a fire drifting from behind them. Shortly afterward he was close enough to make out several men and horses. And as he closed the distance he thought he recognized Early Jordan standing alongside a downed knee-thick spruce log talking to a burly, thickset man, gesticulating as though in anger.

Bill came aground now and stood with hand resting lightly on the claybank's nose, ready to choke off a whicker should some animal below signal his presence. He moved off to his left behind a spruce and was kneeling there when he heard Early shout, "You do it my way, not yours. You've wasted the best log we've cut."

Bill smiled sparely, sensing in the old man's tone a note of harassment, of inadequacy. He was glad now that he had risked coming here, though it took him all of ten minutes to study the five men of Jordan's crew and be fairly certain he had never before seen any of them.

At the end of that interval he led the claybank on down through the trees and straight toward the fire. One man looked up, saw him and went on with his work of trimming a log, showing no apparent interest. The man Early had been arguing with was the next to notice him, and this one also looked away with no curiosity or sign of recognition.

Heartened by this, Bill took the claybank almost as far as the burned-down fire before stopping and calling, "Where's Jordan?"

Early, on his knees and working one end of a crosscut saw ten yards distant, jerked his head around with an expression of outright amazement. Bill was quick to speak again. "Anyone know where I can find the boss?"

"Right here." Early had his wits about him now and, coming erect, spoke in his usual gruff way.

Bill looked at him. "Burgess tells me you're needing help. I'm hired to build your sleds."

"Now are you?" Early came as far as the far side of the fire, seeing that two of the others, having listened to this interchange, were once again going about their work. And now the old man played his part by asking testily, "So you just take over, eh? What makes Burgess think you know how to put a sled together?"

"Because I've done it before."

"Have you looked over those engines we're hauling?"

When Bill nodded, Early half turned and motioned to the nearest of three big logs. "Think ones like that'll do?"

"They will if they're long enough."

The old man glanced beyond Bill then, scowling. "We'd have four good ones if I didn't have a man with a brain so lame he cut one in two to make cross pieces."

"Now see here." Bill turned at the sound

166

of a gruff voice behind him to find the man Early had been arguing with leaning on a double-bitted axe glowering at the old man. "I was whittling timber before you —"

"Just you get on with what you were told to do, McBride," Early cut in. "Unless you want to pull out and draw your wages."

McBride turned sullenly back to his work of lopping branches from the stem of a smaller spruce. And Early picked this moment to come around the fire, saying, "Let's you and me get our heads together, stranger."

As he came in alongside Bill he spoke more quietly. "You son of a gun, you're askin' for it coming here."

"I've never set eyes on any of these men before, Early."

"Suppose they have on you, though?"

"That's a chance I take. So let's get on with this." As an afterthought, Bill added, "By the way, you can call me Adams."

Early sighed worriedly, saying nothing. That was the beginning of four hours of hard work for Bill. At the outset he squatted near the fire while he traced out the plan of one of the big sleds in the snow. There would be three main runner logs flattened and grooved along the bottoms, with four cross braces to be notched into the main logs and so bolted into position that they would be wedged against the engine's three pairs of drive wheels. Finally, the engine would be chained to the sled front and back.

Once Early objected, "That's one sweet load to pull up a steep grade. We got the teams, but how do we handle them all strung out the way they'll be and fighting harness?"

"By hauling from both front corners of the sled, using two separate sets of doubletrees. That gives you teams working abreast, say four on a side. And the same at the back."

"At the back?" Early echoed in strong bewilderment. "How?"

"Cut your middle log twenty feet longer than the side runners. Bolt a crosspiece on its end, then rig your doubletrees from the ends of the cross log. That'll give you two teams on each side of your center runner pulling from behind."

The old man whistled softly in admiration of the idea. "Who thought that up?"

Bill didn't answer, didn't tell Jordan that this was his own notion for handling such an awkward, heavy weight without the teams being unmanageable. He went on now to explain the details of how each of the main runner logs and crosspieces were to be secured by two one-inch bolts at each joining, then how the runners were to be tallowed. They discussed the use of chain block and tackle to help the teams up the steepest grades, the proper way to snub either end of the big sled to swing it around narrow bends.

Finally Early stood up once more, looking down at Bill. "Now I think it can be done. For the first time I'm sure, dead sure."

"You've got to be, Early."

The work went on, with the two best axe-men presently put to flattening one side of the longest log, the center runner. It was after this work was well started that Early caught McBride using a wedge to split one of the other runner logs.

Bill heard the beginning of this second argument, saw that Early was raging. He hurried over there, forgetting himself as he took a hold on one of the old man's arms and pulled him away from the damaged log and McBride. "Easy, Early. There's more where this one came from."

Only after he had spoken did he realize that he had called Early by name. It was obvious that McBride noticed this, though a moment later as the old man swore at him he seemed to forget what he had heard, drawling, "Easy, you old coot, or I belt you one."

"No you won't. Because you're fired as of now."

McBride, eyeing Jordan and then Bill, tossed the sledge hammer aside. "Fair enough.

Only don't ask me back when the job bogs down."

"You're what's bogging us down. Who ever heard of splitting a log to flatten it?"

McBride favored Early with one more belittling glance before he walked over to where the crew's horses were tied beyond the fire. Early and Bill watched him ride away in the gathering dusk toward the pass road, Bill now fairly sure that if McBride had noticed anything it didn't mean much.

"When's quitting time, Early?"

"Six. What'll you do, just ride off?"

Bill nodded. "Right about now. You can tell the others I had to get in to see Burgess about something."

"Do I see you tomorrow?"

"Maybe, but probably not. You're set on everything for the up haul." Frowning in thought a long moment, Bill added, "Tell you what. If I can't get to you before you've made your first haul to the top of the pass, I'll see you there. No matter what time of day or night it is. Lets see . . ."

He thought back upon yesterday morning, trying to remember details of the country he had ridden up along Dead Man before meeting Akers below. All at once he recalled something. "There's a high ridge smack at the head of the pass to the west. Halfway up the ridge you'll see a big dead tree lying against a ledge with its roots sticking up plain enough to spot from the road. There's where I'll be."

"Play it careful, Bill. And if it looks risky, keep away. I've got this thing in my noodle now, got it good. Damned if I want to be sitting in at your wake."

"Then we'll see how it works out."

Bill went to the fire and stood a good five minutes thoroughly warming himself, thinking that with only one skimpy meal in him so far today he would ride deep into the higher hills and risk a fire again tonight so as to eat well before turning in.

He left the camp without anyone noticing, for the light was fading fast, letting him barely make out the men working beyond the fire. Just to play it safe, he made a pretense of heading for the road.

The claybank had carried him a scant two hundred yards when suddenly a voice off to his left called, "Tenn, hoist your hands."

Bill's frame went rigid and his head came around to make out McBride's wide shape standing beside his horse barely thirty feet away. Though he couldn't see it, he knew that the man's hand fisted a gun.

For a moment an overpowering sense of helplessness, of vast disappointment, turned Bill weak. But then a nerveless calm rid him of all emotion and he asked tonelessly, "Ten? Ten of what?"

McBride had dropped the reins and, walking in on him now, chuckled dryly. "A good try, Tenn. But not good enough." He came on several more strides before he added, "This is better than I'd hoped for. Now I collect a reward. Did you hear about that? The town's put up three hundred so far."

The man was coming in on him as Bill said, "You've got something twisted, mister. A reward? What's that got to do with me?"

McBride was close enough now, directly below, to let Bill see his down-lipped smile. "Just keep those hands like they are while I de-horn you, Tenn."

This claybank was a quick-witted cutting horse, sensitive to rein and knee and spur. And now as McBride reached up and started drawing the Winchester from the boot under Bill's leg, holding a Colt's lined in his other hand, Bill lifted his off boot wide and let it fall hard to rowel the horse viciously in the barrel.

One instant his rangy frame was sitting loosely, hands at the level of his shoulders. The next the saddle erupted violently to one side, then upward with a slam that jarred his spine.

The rifle spun outward and down as the

claybank rammed into McBride. Bill twisted his upper body away, doubling over. Mc-Bride's gun exploded deafeningly the split-second the horn jarred his shoulder.

He felt the blast pound his hipbone. He drove home both spurs and the big animal lunged ahead, momentarily breaking stride, stumbling over an object in the snow underfoot. A hoarse, agonized scream sounded from below then as Bill lay flat to the saddle, feeling the claybank go on smoothly.

Reining first to one side and then the other, he felt his horse stretch out to a full run. A second explosion thundered out of the night behind him, echoing away across the hills to deaden the muffled pound of the claybank's hooves. The pain, the deep ache in his hip was beginning to come as he topped a rise and ran the gelding on down through the pines.

V

The cold cut like a knife and the snow was falling lightly at dawn the second morning after Bill Tenn had ridden down McBride to slip back into the hills.

Across in Granite, Early Jordan and his crew and teams were at work well before it was light, hauling the two sleds they had finished late yesterday — one much longer than the other — to the end of a siding where a snow-covered Mogul with a cold firebox and an empty boiler stood waiting to be loaded.

Last evening Burgess had decided that the first haul across Dead Man would be a single load, an engine without its tender. And now while a yard gang dismantled the log bumper at the siding's end, Early and his men rode the smaller sled across to the tunnel warehouse to load screwjacks, crow bars, spikes and heavy chain.

Although none of them knew it, Sam Akers had come across here last night for two reasons. First, he wanted to see the start of the rumored haul of the Mogul. But, more important, as a result of his furtive visit the man

Early had known as McBride had boarded the five o'clock southbound local this morning, with money in pocket and on his way to a friendlier country that would let him mend his four broken ribs and collarbone and perhaps forget what it felt like to be trampled by a seventeen-hand horse.

At about the time Sam Akers was eating his breakfast in the hotel in Granite, shortly after eight o'clock, Sheila Flynn came up Pinetop's Alder Street wearing a heavy coat, high overshoes and her mother's fringed shawl tied under chin and covering her chestnut hair. Wading the deep drifts, she stopped twice to speak to men shovelling the path, and another time to commiserate with the owner of the feed store whose wooden awning had last night buckled under the weight of the new snow.

Further on, she turned in at the door of John Updyke's office. Coming into the room, a swirl of snow following her, she was confronted by the incongruous sight of the lawyer standing beyond his desk next to the stove holding a heavy book in gloved hands, a thick wool muffler wound about his neck.

She burst out laughing. "John, what a sight."

"Don't think it's funny." Updyke exhaled strongly, breathing out a misty vapor. "Had the fire built in here before six and you can still see your breath." He came across to take her arm and lead her back to the stove. "Better keep your coat on."

She pulled the shawl back across her shoulder and unbuttoned the coat, holding it open to the stove's feeble warmth. John Updyke's glance took in her slenderness and the high coloring of her cheeks, and he said in genuine admiration, "No one's got any right to look as pretty as you so early of a bitter day, girl."

She made him a small curtsy. "Use that kind of flattery on all your clients and you'll wind up as judge one day. But thank you anyway."

His thin face took on a sober look. "You a client? Or is it . . ." His pause was deliberate. "Or has Mary seen you as I asked her to?"

"You're good at guessing. Yes, that's why I'm here."

Sheila's tone had been grave and now he asked simply, "Well?"

She shook her head, "Mom and I can't make head or tail of it. Why would Buck and Sam be talking about silver, and claims? It . . . it's even harder for me to believe than it is for mom."

"Why should that be?"

"Because of something Sam said the morning of the funeral. He was wishing he could have been around the night before when Buck was killed. If he had been, he said, they'd have buried Tenn along with Buck."

Updyke's expression showed nothing beyond polite surprise. When he didn't speak, she went on, "It was a foolish thing to say, of course. And I know how it sounds, putting it alongside what Mary knows. Yet mom thinks it's perfectly natural Sam shouldn't tell us of having been with Buck on the street that night."

The lawyer's bony shoulders lifted, fell. "Perhaps it is."

"You, too? Why? You think he doesn't want to hurt our feelings by telling us he and Buck had a run-in?"

"That'd be my guess. They were close friends. Akers is probably hating himself for crossing Buck, since it turned out the way it did. Give the man credit for letting sleeping dogs lie."

"I'd rather he came out and admitted the whole thing."

"Then ask him about it. As a matter of fact I wish you would. This thing's been on my mind and I'd like it cleared up."

She gave him a troubled look. "It's . . . I'm almost afraid to ask him. Afraid he'll lie just to spare my feelings. John, I've grown fond of that man. Or I had, let's say."

"There are ways you could put it to him without his knowing."

Sighing audibly, Sheila murmured, "Maybe I will. But there's something else. Red Bushrod stopped around last night. I had . . . He gave me a bad few mintues."

"Red isn't the only one wondering what happened there in the jail. He's blamed me for smuggling that gun in to Bill. Did you own up that it was you?"

"No." Sheila smiled guiltily. "A woman can always make excuses with a man like Red. I've been so ashamed of what I did that I . . . just pretended I didn't know what he was talking about. He's nice and didn't press me too hard."

"Meaning I shouldn't either?"

"You're different, John. We're old friends."

At his dour look, she went on, "Mary could have told you but promised she wouldn't. I went to the jail to . . . to use Buck's gun on Tenn. But then when it came to the point of doing it, I couldn't. There's something about him I . . ."

When she hesitated, John Updyke solemnly stated, "Yes, there is something about him. There's a whole lot about Bill to let you know he could never have killed Buck. He's a fine man, Sheila, with more downright honest guts than anyone I've ever come across."

She wasn't looking at him now as she held her hands out to the stove's warmth. "I did get as far as trying what I'd set out to do, as far as pointing the gun at him. But then he threw a blanket at me. It was the blanket jarring my hand that pulled the trigger. Now . . . now I'm almost glad he got away."

"Some day you'll be more than almost glad."

Her glance swung around to meet his. "Do you know what happened to him night before last? That he was hurt, that —"

"Do I know it?" he cut in harshly. He paced the three-step distance to his desk, then turned on her. "Haven't I been half off my head since yesterday when I got the word from old Jordan that they found blood along Bill's track the other night? And the fool who shot him claims he couldn't have missed."

"Then you think he may be . . ."

"Dead?" The lawyer shook his head savagely. "No, won't let myself."

"Isn't there a way of your finding him, John?"

"Maybe. Just maybe. But if I try to get to him I give him away. Friend Akers has seen to that."

"Sam? I don't understand."

"You've heard about Akers' try at Bill up on the pass the other morning?" At her nod, he went on caustically, "It seems he's convinced Bushrod that sooner or later I'll try and get in touch with Bill again, which happens to be true. So Red's warned me he's having me watched. Which means my hands are tied."

"John, let me go to him, to Bill."

Her intense, unexpected words visibly jarred the lawyer. For a moment he eyed her in disbelief. Then a derisive quality tinged his glance. "So you can finish what you started the other night?"

Sheila's eyes showed shock and hurt. "How long have we known each other?" she asked, barely audibly.

"For as long as I can remember. But that doesn't cut any ice now."

"Do you trust me?"

"Trust has nothing to do with this. You think Bill clubbed Buck. I happen to think he didn't."

"Would you believe me if I told you I've changed my mind about him?" Reading his doubting look, Sheila insisted, "I realize how this must sound after what I did the other night. Yet it happens to be true. Why, I can't explain. But you have to believe me. I came here to find out if you could tell me anything about him. Now that I know how things stand, I'm asking you to let me help."

John Updyke was almost glowering at her and his voice trembled as he countered,

"You're a woman and a damned fine one. But we're forgetting that now. We're playing with a man's life."

"We're maybe saving a man's life, John."

Her quiet-spoken words broke the dam of John Updyke's doubt. One moment that doubt was strong, the next none whatsoever remained. Sighing heavily, he said, "Say I do believe you. Even so, you couldn't help. It'd be all a man could do to ride into that back country in weather like this. There'd be grub to pack in, and a rifle. If Bill's badly hurt he'd either have to be brought out or Doc Serles would have to go in to him."

"Remember what a tomboy I once was?" Sheila quietly asked. "You know I've ridden weather as bad as this, even camped out in it. Let me do this, John. It's my one way of making it up to Bill."

The lawyer eyed her speculatively, almost coldly a long moment. Then, suddenly deciding something, he nodded. "All right, you asked for it." His tone was edged with frustration, near-anger. "Do you remember Pace's logging camp up on Baldy?"

"Do I? Didn't dad help build that big cabin for Pace? Haven't I been up there a dozen times either with dad or Buck?"

"That was years ago, Sheila. The road's gone now, brushed over —"

"But there are tree blazes all the way. I can get there. I'll take him food, Buck's rifle. And what medicine and bandages we have at the house, just in case. I'll start right away."

Sheila was buttoning her coat now, her eyes bright with eagerness as she tied the scarf about her head once more. "You're to tell him what Mary's told us," Updyke inserted. "Also that Jordan should be making his start up the pass road with the first engine sometime today. Tell him to stay away, that the old man can handle everything."

She nodded, stepping across to him now to take his hand. "John, I'll never forget this. Thank you for trusting me."

"You're the one who's got the thanks coming." He was more his old self now, there was a mildness in his tone and a gentleness in his eyes. "Be careful, girl. Tell Bill . . ." He shrugged, his homely face relaxing into a smile. "You'll know what to say."

She went quickly to the door and, opening it, looked back at him. "Oh, something else, John. Mary Stone thinks you're about the nicest man she ever met."

Her eyes were bright with mischievousness and she laughed softly at seeing how red his face became. And with that parting word having revived their old closeness, she left the room.

Going back down the street she was wondering what she could tell her mother to keep her from being curious as to where she was going. Even more important, she knew she couldn't risk going to the livery to hire a horse, for that would only rouse curiosity that might give her trouble.

By the time she reached home she had decided to borrow Higgins', the neighbor's, roan mare. She would also borrow his saddle, ride man-fashion and wear her divided wool skirt. She would meantime be thinking up some plausible reason to give Mrs. Higgins for wanting to borrow the animal.

She had been hoping that her mother would be working in the kitchen, that she could go upstairs and change her clothes without Brigid Flynn knowing. But she had no sooner closed the door than her mother was calling from upstairs, "That you, Sheila?"

"Yes, mom." Sheila hung the shawl and her coat on the umbrella-stand rack by the door.

She was taking off her overshoes when her mother called down again. "There's something here I want you to see, something of Buck's."

Sheila climbed the stairs and went on back to Buck's room to find Brigid Flynn standing by the bureau beyond the bed. The older woman gestured to an assortment of odds and ends lying on the bureau top. "I've finally gotten around to going through the things they found in Buck's pockets. See what you make of this."

She held out a dog-eared square of paper almost worn through along its smudged folds. Looking down at it, Sheila gave a start. For the first thing that caught her eye was the word *Claim* lettered along the paper's lower edge.

Above the word a double curving line ran obliquely up and across the paper bearing the legend, *Road*. It bisected a square at each corner of which was pencilled a meaningless number.

When Sheila's wide-eyed glance lifted, Brigid Flynn tilted her head in a slow nod. "It seems Mary wasn't so wrong after all. Sheila, that's the plan of a claim."

Bill Tenn opened his eyes and lay staring at the bunkhouse roof joists for a solid minute, wondering if he should try to move, deciding not to just yet. His head was clear, he felt less feverish than he had yesterday. Best of all, something he scarcely dared believe was that his right hipbone no longer throbbed with that knifing pain of yesterday but was merely sore now.

Yesterday and the night before had been

a seemingly endless torment. Last night, feeling giddy and about to lose grip of his senses, he had listened to a small voice of reason telling him that he must do something more than simply trust that the deep puncture through the flesh of his hip would eventually heal.

He had carried wood in here, built a fire and heated his clasp-knife. With the blade's point still red hot, he had cut deep into the wound. He had later picked out two splinters of bone and finally staunched the flow of blood with snow and a clean handkerchief. Now he knew that it had been the right thing.

Rolling his head around, he stared out the nearby window to see big flakes of snow dropping steadily out of a leaden sky. He had no way of telling what time it was, though he supposed it must be late, perhaps as late as noon. He had slept away the fever and his exhaustion and now he was suddenly ravenously hungry, unable to remember when he had last put anything into his stomach besides snow melt.

He threw the blankets down and rolled gently onto his good side, feeling a tightness and a soreness in his other hip, but little else. Holding his bad leg stiff, he came awkwardly erect with the help of a forked aspen sapling he had cut yesterday to use as a makeshift crutch.

The cold hit him sharply and he hurried to pull on his coat. He was stooping over to reach some small branches from the stack of wood he had carried in here late yesterday when the claybank tied in the lee of the sawdust bin across the clearing whickered loudly.

His nerves drew instantly tight. Thrusting the crutch back under his arm, he swung in fast, broken strides toward the window. Halfway to it he lurched heavily around as an animal beyond the door in back of him suddenly neighed in answer to the claybank.

He crossed to the far wall alongside the door in a series of awkward lunges, trying to hold his right leg stiff, the effort leaving him short of breath. He reached to his belt and lifted out Buck Flynn's big Colt's, flattening his back to the log wall now and edging over until he could scan the stretch of drifted ground between the bunkhouse and the aspens below. He saw Sheila Flynn leading a roan mare in on the door.

The near-panic that had gripped him drained slowly away. Letting the gun fall so that he could grip the crutch with that hand, he hobbled around and into the doorway.

Sheila saw him and stopped barely twenty feet away, close enough to let him see her warm smile and the gladness and relief in her eyes as she breathed, "So I've found you."

"You have. But how?"

His flat words erased her smile. "John Updyke," she quietly answered.

He saw that she was chilled in spite of her heavy coat and wool skirt, yet he thrust aside that awareness as he tonelessly queried, "Has John gone *loco?* Or did you trick it out of him?"

"I didn't." She noticed the gun in his hand and nodded to it. "You won't need that."

Bill glanced briefly down at the weapon. "It's the one you used on me the last time. Why wouldn't I need it now?"

"Because I've come here to help . . . Because I know now how wrong I've been about you."

His beard-shadowed face relaxed in disbelief. Just now he saw the rifle on the roan's saddle and, trusting this girl not at all, drawled, "Is that why you lugged along the Winchester? Don't bother —"

"But John asked me to bring it. He knew you'd lost yours the other night."

Sheila dropped the reins and started toward him, then halted abruptly as she saw the Colt's start to lift. "Please, Bill. What can I say to make you believe me?"

If John did send her you're playing the fool. Quite suddenly Bill did believe her. He brought up the gun and dropped it in the pocket of his coat, feeling warm inside now, a haunting weight all at once gone from his mind. "You don't have to say one thing," he told her with a sheepish grin. "I'll just turn around and you can boot me one."

Sheila's smile returned instantly, radiantly. But it was short-lived as she came up to him, able now to make out the haggard look of his face. "They were right," she breathed softly. "That man didn't miss the other night."

"No. But I've got a tough hide."

Sheila came in beside him, looking up and studying his face in a way that made him say awkwardly, "Give me a couple more days and I'll be mended." He moved aside and gestured into the room behind him. "What was it the spider said to the fly? Something about a parlor. This isn't one, but you're welcome anyway."

He liked the lilt of her laugh and her nearness roused an awe and excitement in him that was momentarily unsettling as she looked across the long, empty room to the drifted snow and the ashes of his last night's fire at its far end, then to the gaping hole in the roof above.

"It's colder than an ice house. Why haven't you a fire going?"

"Hadn't wanted to run the chance of anyone smelling the smoke and paying me a visit. But a minute ago I'd decided to build one anyway."

"Then let's get at it. I'm frozen and so must you be."

Over the next few minutes Bill clumsily tried to help her. Yet she had broken a handful of twigs and shredded some tinder-dry bark almost before he could reach down for them. Once the twigs had caught she went outside and dragged a small dead windfall to the door, kicking off the stubborn big branches and heaping them on the fire until he warned her, "Don't let's burn the place down."

Her smile came once again, but only briefly. As she turned from the blaze there was a troubled look in her eyes. "How long since you've eaten, Bill?"

"Almost forget when it —"

"And where is it you're hurt? That comes first," Seeing him lay hand on hip, she said, "Let me see it."

"Now look here. I'm not shedding my clothes in front of —"

"Yes you are. Let me see it."

With a deep sigh, he opened the coat and unbuckled his belt. "You Irish are a stubborn tribe."

"We Irish are a lot more than stubborn."

He pulled the shirt out of his pants, opened the slit he had cut in his underwear at midnight

189

night before last. For some odd reason, now that he had forced himself to it, he wasn't embarrassed even slightly at laying bare the blood-stiffened handkerchief and the flesh of his hipbone.

Sheila caught her breath at sight of the blood, then gently tried to lift the bandage and look underneath. But when it wouldn't come away she straightened. "It's not red and it looks like we ought to let it alone. I've brought along clean cloth and soap and peroxide. You can use them when you need them." Looking up at him, she said gently, "It must have hurt like the devil."

When he only arched his brows, carefully pushing the tail of the shirt down inside his belt again, she turned to the door. "Now for some food. Mom sent along part of a ham. And I raided Higgins' chicken house for eggs right off the nest. Would that do for a start, along with coffee?"

"Sheila."

She was halfway through the door when his sharp word stopped her. And as she looked around he asked in an awed way, "Are you telling me your mother knows you're here, wanted you to come?"

"She knows I'm somewhere seeing you, Bill. And, yes, I suppose you could say she wanted me to come. It's . . . it'll take her time to come around to believing as I do. But she's willing."

Sheila leaned against the doorframe. "There are some things you can't know. I don't think John's had the chance to tell you what Mary Stone heard on the street the night Buck was killed."

"No. Who's Mary Stone?"

"Someone I trust and like. Here's what you don't know." Sheila repeated what Mary had told her yesterday, told him of her talk with John Updyke this morning, all the while holding his sharp attention until she finished by saying, "So on the way up here I was doing something, asking myself the same questions mom's asking. First about that drawing for a claim location, and about the silver. Then about Buck. If you didn't kill him, who did?"

"Akers?"

Her brows went up in a questioning look. "It's possible, I'll admit. But I can't believe it, can't begin to. Look what losing Buck is already costing Sam. Fred Stone tells Mary that nothing's gone right at the tunnel these last few days. Sam can't find a man to handle that crew. But what sticks in my mind over everything else is that Sam and Buck were such close friends, really close."

"Who else had a grudge to work off against Buck?"

"Several men. You don't keep a crew like the one at the tunnel in line without making enemies. Buck had to whip several —"

Suddenly Sheila was looking beyond Bill with a wide-eyed stare of alarm. He wheeled quickly around and his high frame stiffened in shock at what he saw.

Sam Akers was standing outside the empty window laying a rifle across its sill.

Sheila cried softly, "No!" to erase the beginning of a doubt in Bill, for it had flashed across his mind that she might have planned this with Akers.

The big man's curl-brim hat and the shoulders of his coat were dusted white with snow. His cold-reddened face wore a look of disbelief, of affront now as he said hoarsely, "My God, Sheila. This is hard to believe."

"Sam, put that gun down."

Akers was as openly amazed as Bill at the intentness of Sheila's tone. "Put it down? Why? I'm taking this killer back to jail."

"You're not, Sam. You have to —"

Sam Akers was staring so intently, so disbelievingly, at Sheila that he didn't notice the beginning of Bill's sideward lunge. Only when Bill's crutch thudded to the floor was he aware of his mistake in having let his attention stray. His glance whipped around and his thumb drew back the rifle's hammer as he jerked the weapon quickly around.

But then Bill's gun settled into line with him and he froze motionless, the rifle still wide of its target.

"Drop it, Akers."

For a moment it appeared that Sam Akers' humiliation and high anger would drive him beyond the point of reason. But then common sense made him loosen his grip on the Winchester, letting it fall from the sill to the dirt floor below the window. His outraged glance swung to Sheila and he intoned in a trembling voice, "Wait'll the town hears this."

Bill stooped to pick up the crutch now and with it under his arm again he limped toward the window, motioning with the Colt's. "Turn your back."

Akers' look was ugly. He was deliberate in facing around, and his massive body stiffened at the touch of Bill's hand, at feeling the Colt's under his coat leave its holster. Then Bill told him, "Move off."

Bill could hear Sheila coming in behind him as Akers stepped on out across the open ground. Without looking around he told her, "I'd give anything if this hadn't happened," for he was only now fully realizing what this past minute had meant to her.

"So would I. But it has happened and we make the best of it." He was once again aware of her closeness as she came to stand beside him and look out at Akers. Then abruptly she was asking, "Can you ride, Bill?"

Akers had stopped and was facing the window once more, his look turning sardonic, mean as he saw them standing there. Because of that look, Bill said, "I can. But can I leave you with him?"

"Of course. I'll . . . This is my affair from now on. Only first I want to be sure about you. Where will you go?"

"Any one of half a hundred places," he answered.

"Then I'll get your horse." He noticed a helpless, hurt quality in her glance as, eyeing Akers, she hesitantly added, "Bill, he would have killed you. That was a . . . a fine thing you did, not shooting just then."

When he made no comment, she turned and left him and in another few seconds he saw her running across to the ruin of the big bin where the claybank was tied. Akers observed this in glowering silence until Sheila was leading the animal back toward the bunkhouse. He looked at Bill then to say flatly, "I'll hunt you down if it takes a week or a year, Tenn."

Over the next five minutes Sheila did most of the work, for as she came back into the cabin she told Bill, "You'll have to watch him

194

while I do this other." She rolled the tarp and blankets and tied them to Bill's saddle while he stood at the window eyeing Akers. He had it in mind to carry the saddle out and put it on the claybank, yet she had finished that chore before he was aware of it. Last of all she went to the roan, carried across the sack of provisions she had brought and tied them to his saddle, afterward coming to the door to tell him, "You'd better be on your way."

He emptied Akers' Colt's and the rifle, only then leaving the window and carrying them across to the door where she waited. His look was gentle, somewhat awed as he came up to her. "A man never knows where he has friends. This is something I'll always remember, Sheila."

"And it's something I will, too. Be careful, Bill. Be very careful."

He gave way to a strong impulse then and reached out and laid a hand on her shoulder, squeezing it, smiling down at her. A wondering, utterly grave expression came to her eyes as he turned away, limped across to the claybank and awkwardly pulled his high frame astride the leather.

"Sure you'll be all right?"

She nodded, that softness and gravity still in her eyes as she said, barely audibly, "Luck, Bill."

195

He lifted a hand in a spare gesture of farewell and reined the claybank toward the trees. Just before he reached them he looked back, not at Sheila but at Akers, and tossed the big man's Colt's and rifle into the snow.

Sheila watched him until the silvery grey mass of the aspens had swallowed his shape, vaguely aware of Akers rounding the near end of the cabin and coming toward her. And in another moment his harsh voice intruded upon this somehow hallowed moment:

"Now you'll do some explaining, Sheila."

His words grated against her mood, instantly rousing her anger so that when she faced him, her eyes were bright with rebellion. She said nothing, and he halted two strides from her, hands on hips as he looked down to meet her defiant glance. "I knew there was something queer about it from the first minute I sighted you up there on Dead Man. From when I saw you cut off the road and head this way."

It took her a deliberate moment to see something in his words. "Then you followed me all this way instead of calling out and riding with me? Why?"

"I said it looked queer from the beginning."

"Then you don't trust me?"

"Trust you? Good Lord, look what's happened. Look what I found you doing." He was on uncertain ground and knew it as he added defensively, "Trust has nothing to do with this."

"It would if it was the other way about, Sam," she quietly told him. "It would if you'd done this, not me."

"But why did you do it?"

"Because I don't think Bill is guilty of what he stood trial for."

" 'Bill', is it?" Carefully, pointedly, Akers asked, "What's between you two that I don't know about?"

"There's nothing between us."

"You were here alone with him. You've had a fire going and you looked cozy enough."

Sheila's face took on color. "Sam, there's something foul in the mind of any man who would suspect or even hint of such a thing."

"Why?" he blazed. "Tenn's a wanted man, isn't he? He killed your brother, didn't he? Now you —"

"I've already said I don't believe he killed Buck."

Akers' eyes veiled over in a wary way. "If he didn't, then who did?"

There was an instant when she was remembering her conversation with John Updyke this morning, remembering the lawyer having said that she must ask Akers about being on the street with Buck the night of the killing.

This fact was the root of her belief in Bill Tenn's innocence, this and her instinct for knowing that Bill was incapable of killing. Yet just now she was warned by what she had already noticed in Akers this morning, a hint of brutality she had never before glimpsed in him, not to pick this moment for a showdown with him.

So she answered evasively, "I don't quite know yet. But some day I will know."

The big man shook his head in a gesture of utter bafflement. "You don't leave a man a thing to hang onto. Here I think I'm doing the right thing, doing it for Buck's sake, and you set me back on my heels with some confounded thing I don't even begin to understand."

All at once Sheila thought of a way of explaining. "Sam, I thought I was doing the right thing the other night when I went to the jail. Went there to kill Bill. We haven't had a chance to talk about that. What happened was . . . I had the gun pointed at him, was ready to pull the trigger. But I couldn't. Something about him told me he . . . that he could never kill a man the way Buck was killed. Or any other way unless he was driven to it to save his own life."

"Who says he couldn't? Why, he tried to rob me, didn't he?"

His indignation lacked conviction. Noticing that and still feeling the aftermath of the strong physical impact of Bill Tenn's presence, Sheila was all at once wanting to end this pointless interchange. She said lifelessly, "Don't try and understand what I've done then, Sam. Just lay it to a woman's whim, anything. But don't . . ."

His anger seemed to be weakening for the first time then as he said almost gently, "This is the damnedest thing I've ever come across. It's wrecking something we shouldn't let it wreck."

A measure of the near-forgotten fondness she had felt for this big man stirred in her now and she told him, "Give me time. Time to know my own mind. And until I do know it, be patient with me, Sam." Listlessly, she asked, "Will you ride back to town with me?"

"I'd ride anywhere with you, Sheila. You know that." Glumly, still confused and unsure of himself, Sam Akers left her to walk on across to his rifle and handgun lying in the snow near the trees.

By mid-afternoon, Early Jordan and his crew had learned much about handling their teams and the big sled with its towering load that continually threatened to take the bit of every mare and gelding in its iron teeth and go where it chose.

They were taught their hardest lessons on the lower, gentler grades of the Dead Man road where mistakes weren't too costly. The nearest they came to disaster was once when the sled, rounding a tight bend too fast, swung its middle log runner so sharply that a mare pulling with the teams back there went down in a tangle of harness and was pushed unharmed over a steep bank so that she hung and had to be cut loose. After making repairs, they walked the teams around the bends.

Once they began pulling the steeper grades the deep snow piled in front of the sled to block the runner logs so often that the teamsters spent almost as much time swinging scoop shovels as they did handling the reins. It was past four o'clock, the light was fading and the sky was still spilling its seemingly endless load of snow upon the timbered slope when Early miserably observed,

"If this storm don't let up we shovel our way over the mountain."

It was shortly after he had spoken those caustic words and had begun to worry about the pass being snowed completely shut during the night that he suddenly thought of something Bill had told him two days ago. He let out a whoop of joy, yelling, "A plow! Hell, why didn't I think of it sooner?"

He sent two men into the nearby pines in search of a tree big enough to split to make a wedge plow. In almost exactly one more hour he and two other men had rigged the two halves of a split pine log flat sides out, braced by two crosspieces and with a pair of doubletrees at the front where the two halves joined in a V. By then a supper fire was thinning the blackness a hundred yards above. Two teams were hitched to the plow and pulled it easily up the road, leaving such a clean packed path that two or three of the men cheered lustily as it pulled even with the cook's fire.

Not a man grumbled over the majority's decision to work on into the night. They seemed to have caught Early's excitement, his conviction that something they had at first thought nearly impossible of accomplishment now wasn't at all impossible. They had easily pulled a particularly steep stretch of lower road late in the afternoon, and once they had finished the meal and were talking idly afterward, listening to the snow hiss into the leaping flames, one man solemnly stated, "I've a dollar says we have this contraption on Cedar Street by this time tomorrow night."

The rest remained silent for several moments, until a second teamster observed, "No takers, Josh."

"Bet I get some takers for this." A tall, gangling man left the fire, walked on out to the engine's towering shape beyond and climbed to its varnished cab.

He came back down with a jug dangling from one hand. Uncorking it as he walked in on the fire, he noticed that Early was frowning, not liking this. So he first offered it to the old man, drawling, "One good swig apiece between us, no more. When it's made the rounds, we put the cork back. Now drink up, Jordan."

A slow smile broke across Early Jordan's face, erasing his worry. He tilted the jug, swallowed deeply and passed it on. Not one among them took undue advantage of this unlooked-for treat, and within five more minutes the Mogul's headlight was blazing a white path up the snowy road and they were back at work again.

The whiskey seemed to seal their mood of willingness, and that first hour after they started on again it was hard for Early, driving the plow, to keep well ahead in the headlight's glare. The plow made the going three times as fast as it had been, and during that hour they stopped only once to shovel the big runners clear.

It was shortly after they pulled on once again with gunshot cracks of the teamsters' bull whips that two riders came down along the road and turned in to have a word with Early, who was taking a rest, riding the sled and sitting with his back to one of the engine's big drive wheels.

"You Jordan?" the lead rider asked, walking his animal slowly alongside. At Early's nod, he announced, "Bushrod sent us across to keep you company."

The old man smiled smugly. "Does he think Bill would be fool enough to show up anywhere around here?"

"That's the general idea. He did it three days ago, didn't he?"

"Then stick around. Only," Early cautioned severely, "stay out of our way. We got work to do."

The following morning saw the back of the storm broken, until by ten o'clock, as Bill started the climb toward the pass, he could see the silvered timber of the lower hills mottled with patches of brilliant sunlight even though this peak country was still shrouded in heavy cloud.

He rode awkwardly, warily, his weight on the left stirrup. His hip was still sore this morning, though not so tender to touch and movement as it had been yesterday. He had cleaned the wound last night and covered it with a bandage Sheila had brought him, and he was thinking now that if he could get through another day or two without pulling it open the danger of infection would be gone.

This morning seemed far different from recent ones. Seeing Sheila yesterday and learning that he had her respect and understanding had somehow subtly changed his outlook, had made him feel a whole man. His worries had thinned to the point where they no longer seemed so overwhelming. He still felt a sober concern over something going wrong with the hauling of the engine over the pass. Yet the struggle to pay off his debts wasn't so all-important as it had been.

What was important was that he should have the trust and liking of people like Sheila and John Updyke. What was even more important was that he should, probably through both Updyke and Sheila, find a way of clearing his name of the stigma of the trial.

These sobering thoughts stayed with him as he threaded his way into the higher hills, until presently he was once again riding in a comforting thin fog of falling snow that obscured the further ridges and spurs and eased away a measure of his concern over being seen. He was circling to reach the steep timbered face of the high shoulder flanking Dead Man from which he had looked down upon the road the other day, the morning on which Akers had surprised him below as he rode with John Updyke. And in another hour and a half he was sitting the claybank at almost the exact same spot from which he had peered down to make out the fire of Bushrod's two men guarding the pass that morning.

He had hoped to look down from this high vantage point across the twisting miles of road leading to Granite and somewhere see Early Jordan and his crew hauling slowly toward the pass. What he did see surprised him almost beyond belief. Expecting to find the road empty below, Early only well started on the haul up the mountain, he found the big sled with its cumbersome load blocking the road at the beginning of the long downgrade. Figures were milling about it and shortly after he began watching he saw a stage crawl past the big engine and go on in the direction of Granite.

How Early had managed to get this far in such a short space of time confounded him. Yet the fact remained that the old man had somehow accomplished the seemingly impossible. And as the full significance of what he was seeing struck home to him he couldn't hold back a smile of sheer delight.

The distance was too great to let him recognize anyone down there, though in another twenty minutes when he saw two riders go down the road, round a bend that put them out of sight of those above and then start climbing the slope immediately below, he was fairly certain that Jordan was one of the two, the one on the black horse.

If Early had remembered their conversation of three evenings ago, then this was as it should be, for they had arranged a meeting here. But the presence of the second man wasn't as it should be.

It flashed across Bill's mind that Bushrod might be the second rider, that the marshal had somehow discovered his plan for meeting Jordan and that the old man was being brought here with a gun at his back. It also occurred to him that neither of these two was Early.

So he put the claybank on up through the trees toward the crest of the ridge, deciding to take no chances. And from two hundred yards above some five minutes later he looked down through the pines and recognized Early Jordan and Ralph Burgess as they brought their mounts to a stand below the sky-tilted roots of the big windfall he had mentioned to Early the other afternoon.

He put the claybank on down toward them and first the old man, then Burgess, heard him coming and glanced his way. A relieved smile broke across Early's face. The engineer's look was one of stunned, disbelieving amazement.

As Bill came down to them Burgess gave Early a dour glance. "So this is what you had up your sleeve." He unexpectedly smiled then and held out his hand, and as Bill took it he said, "They may lock me up for aiding and abetting a crime, but I have John Updyke's word that you were framed for something you didn't do. Damned if I'm not glad to see you, Tenn. For a couple of reasons."

Early was eyeing Bill more soberly now. "I been up here twice since ten o'clock," he said. "Had about given you up. Bill, did that joker McBride nick you bad?"

"Nothing I won't get over." Bill was noticing the tiredness lining Jordan's thin face and his voice was edged with gentleness as he drawled, "No need to kill yourself getting this done, Early. You must've spent the night at it. Why not wait till tomorrow to start the trip down?"

"Start it? Hell, we're going to finish it today or know the reason why. By this time tomorrow we ought to be on our way up with that coal car and a stack of rails." The old man frowned worriedly, sighing. "But I sure wish you could be down there now, son."

"Trouble?"

Jordan nodded. "The rig started running away with us right after we pulled over the hump. Even with chains wrapped around the runners. So I've got it blocked and there she sits till we figure a way of handling her."

Bill's glance shifted to the engineer, who shrugged eloquently. "Tenn, you'd think I could find a way of helping. We've thought about cables. But we'd be the rest of the winter blocking the sled and taking a new hitch every fifty yards or so."

"Why not rig a stone boat on behind?"

"That'd slide as easy as the big sled," the old man objected.

"It wouldn't if you'd use spikes on the bottom."

Jordan was puzzled. "How's that?"

Bill nodded below. "Isn't that a plow I see down there?"

"Sure is. And if we need spikes, we brought along plenty. But what do we do with them?"

"Nail planks solid along the bottom of your plow. Then drive rows of spikes through your planks and load the plow with as much flat ledge rocks as you need. Say you load it heavy enough so that it takes two good teams to pull it and the sled down your steepest slopes."

Early Jordan glanced surprisedly at Burgess, and the engineer stated dryly, "And here I'm supposed to be able to think out things like this. Why didn't I?"

Bill leaned forward now, resting an elbow

on the horn to ease the weight from his bad leg. "You'll have to watch one thing or you're in real trouble. If your load begins to cut loose, tell your men handling the teams to pull hard for the inside edge of the road."

The old man's eyes were aglow with eagerness as he looked at Burgess. "I'll take that bet now, my friend."

"What bet?" Bill wanted to know.

"On the way up here he wanted to lay me ten dollars to one we wouldn't be in Pinetop by tomorrow night."

"You'll be there tonight," Bill told him. "And if my luck holds I'll be watching from those hills above town."

Dusk was settling over Pinetop that early evening when Sheila borrowed Higgins' roan for the second time in two days and rode less than half a mile up the road and into the glare of the Mogul's headlight to join a throng of townspeople either riding or walking alongside the big sled and its awkward burden. A holiday spirit held the crowd, and there was much loud talk and laughter as it shifted slowly down the road abreast the teams with a man from Early's crew walking on either side keeping the youngsters from jumping onto the big sled.

At first Sheila was confounded at seeing four

209

teams, two on either front corner of the sled, straining to keep the load moving steadily along the downgrade. But then a flaming pitch pine torch carried by one of the crew walking at the back of the sled let her see the rock-loaded plow dragging on behind, and the deep furrows it chewed in the snow. And she all at once understood.

She could sense that the crowd was tense, expectant, and wondered at that until all at once the sled on rounding a steep bend slid sharply sideways toward the road's edge. A wave of alarm ran through her. But the next moment the heavy V-shaped stone sledge chained on behind sharply snubbed the bigger sled. And when the teams pulled steadily on, the Mogul under control again, she cried out in delight to join the ragged cheers of the crowd.

Seeing Early Jordan riding the front corner of the sled now, she let the procession pull on past her, intending to cross to the other side and speak to him. She didn't know the old man but felt an urge to speak to him, to tell him that she had seen Bill yesterday, that his friend wasn't badly hurt.

She was crossing the road when suddenly a voice spoke out of the darkness behind her. "That you, Sheila?"

For a fraction of a second a hard excitement

hit her at the thought that this might be Bill, for he had been in her thoughts just now. But the next instant that emotion died to be replaced by a faint annoyance as she realized it was Sam Akers' voice. And it was with a letdown feeling that she looked around and made out his massive shape astride an animal coming obliquely toward her.

"Hello, Sam."

She knew her tone lacked cordiality but strangely didn't care. He came alongside her and reached out to take her hand, saying quietly, "Sheila, can't we make it up somehow? I'd give a lot if we could both just forget yesterday."

"Then let's do forget it." She touched the roan with spur, moving away from him so that he had to release her hand, saying nervously, "Isn't all this exciting?" The next moment she realized how little reason the big man had to feel as she did, or as the crowd did, and put in awkwardly, "But of course you can't be too happy about it."

Akers laughed dryly. "Suppose I shouldn't be enjoying it, but I am. Why should I mind too much, after all? Working engines at this end only means I finish the job sooner and get on to the next."

Sheila marvelled at his being such a good loser in what was happening tonight, and for a moment she experienced a rebirth of the liking she had felt for him not so many days ago. But then came the sharp recollection of what she knew of the night Buck had died, and that emotion became still-born.

Her nature was so straightforward that even now she gave him the benefit of her doubt, it occurring to her that the big man might still be able to give some perfectly logical and reasonable explanation for not having so far admitted to his encounter with Buck.

She was all at once determined to ask him about it. Yet before she had the chance to speak he was saying gravely, "Speaking of the next job reminds me of something, Sheila. Whatever it turns out to be, it'll probably take me away from here."

She sensed that his words were leading up to something, and a faint feeling of unease was in her as she said, "I suppose it will."

He was once more walking his horse close alongside the mare, and once again reached out to take her hand. "I'm a poor one at mixing together fancy words. So I'll come straight to the point. It's bothered me seeing you slave at cooking for a bunch of paid lodgers, washing and cleaning up after them. I'd like . . . I'd like to take you away from it, Sheila."

She was more embarrassed than surprised at this voicing of his long-expected proposal.

It seemed so clumsy, even callous, that she ignored its import in the face of the indignation that rose in her. "Me, a slave?" She laughed, no merriment whatsoever in her tone. "Sam, the only thing I've ever slaved at in all my life is trying to make it easier for mom, trying to make her happy."

"Don't hold it against a man for choosing the wrong word. I was asking you to marry me."

She saw at once how unfairly she had spoken and was quick to tell him, "It was unkind of me to say that. You're being very nice. But . . ."

"But what?"

Now's the time to ask him. The thought was no sooner with her than she was calmly saying, "There's something I'd like to know first, Sam. About the night Buck died. Did you see him at all that night?"

She felt the sudden probing quality of his glance, and it was a three second interval before he answered, "That night? No. Buck didn't even drop in at the office when he knocked off work for the day." Over another deliberate pause, he queried, "Why should you ask?"

"Call it a woman's curiosity, Sam."

Knowing how unsatisfactory her answer was, she nonetheless didn't qualify it. The finality of his lie came without surprise. Now that he had spoken it she felt an odd sense of relief, and of release. And it was with a feeling akin to real pleasure that she let the weight of her silence bear upon him.

"Wish I knew what you were driving at."

"Nothing, Sam. Nothing."

She saw the big sled outlined in the snow-reflected glare of the engine's headlight now as it crawled around still another turn in the road. And to hide her increasing nervousness she nodded toward it, saying, "Look, they've nearly made it. You can see the lights of the street down there."

All at once she felt the ungentle grip of his big hand on her arm. "Sheila, you'll explain that . . . that about me being with —"

A low, vibrating rumble cut across his words. Someone ahead shouted stridently in alarm. Sheila looked across there to see figures running out from the sled, to see men throwing themselves up through the drifts above the road as the rumble mounted to a pulsating roar.

The bright shaft of the Mogul's ornate headlight suddenly swung crazily to one side, tilted upward. Then, in dread awe, Sheila saw the sled and its burden all at once lurch backward and sink from sight below the level of the road, dragging with it its four fear-crazed teams and the stone-loaded plow.

VI

Bill Tenn followed the Mogul on down off the pass throughout the afternoon, part of the time watching from a ridge a mile away, once peering down from a rim a scant four hundred feet above the road.

As the higher peaks lost the last trace of pinkish sunglow and the sheltering darkness settled over this lower tangle of hills, he rode well ahead of the sled and finally walked the claybank on through the pines flanking the road close above town, wanting to see the engine make its entrance onto the street. He was sitting on a windfall some two hundred yards above the road, watching the lights and the slow-moving procession of onlookers, when the pounding rumble of the caving-in glory hole echoed up to him.

He lunged to a stand, shortening his hold on the reins as the claybank shied nervously. He heard a man shout stridently, saw the headlight's bright shaft sweep suddenly across the fringe of snow-laden pines, then slant sharply skyward.

The sound from below became a low grinding roar. Shouts and cries were blended with it then as the sled and its cumbersome load slid slowly backward and settled into a gaping hole that appeared in the road. His stomach muscles knotted with a sickly feeling as the shrill neighing of the teams echoed up to him, as he watched them being dragged backward into the hole. Then the headlight suddenly went dead and he could see nothing but the pin-point glow of several flares.

Over the next half-minute as more shouts and excited voices sounded from below, his thoughts stayed on dead center. He tensed in sharp apprehension when a gun suddenly exploded once, twice, three times. *There go your teams,* was his disheartening thought as he checked the urge to run down there.

Shortly a brush-fed fire's leaping flames burned a hole in the blackness to light the scene below. He had been thinking of Early Jordan, of the chance that the old man had been riding the sled when the road gave way under it, and over the next few minutes he studied the figures scurrying around the crater, his worry mounting when at the end of that interval he had failed to see his friend.

He was paying no particular attention to a group of half a dozen men standing at the hole's near edge until he saw still another man join them carrying a coil of rope. The newcomer knelt in the snow and tossed the rope downward. Then his pulse slowed at seeing three others of the group take a hold on the rope and pull hard on it.

Suddenly a hatless, dishevelled Early Jordan was dragged over the lip of the crater at the rope's end. And when the old man came to his feet and beat the grime from his coat, Bill let his breath go hoarsely in an exultant cry of thankfulness and relief.

Once Early was moving around in the crowd, apparently little the worse for his close call, Bill's worry eased away and for the first time be began trying to understand what had happened. He was baffled in grasping the fact of a hole of such sizable proportions having gone undiscovered over the many years. The downward angle let him peer into the conical crater and see the engine's half-buried boiler with its diamond stack and sky-slanted headlight. He supposed that the Mogul's cab must be resting some thirty feet below the level of the road.

What confounded him above all was that the road had never given way under far heavier loads than the Mogul and its sled, the countless log loads that had passed over this same spot during the summers when the logging camp on Baldy had been in operation. And now as he looked around in search of some clue that would let him begin to understand the riddle of the cave-in, the feeble glow of the fires at the tunnel camp off to the southeast caught his glance and held it.

Yet he was no sooner struck by the thought that a section of the new tunnel might have fallen in than he was rejecting the notion. For this point along the road, though slightly south of the town's uppermost limits, was still nearly a quarter of a mile out of line with the one he supposed the tunnel should take in boring straight through the mountain to Granite.

His thinking had reached this unsatisfactory stalemate when it occurred to him that he should right now be more concerned over what the accident was costing him than in speculating on the reason for it. He could see two of his geldings lying dead down there in the hole, and he supposed that the other six must certainly have been buried. Sobering as the sight was, it was pointless to look ahead and try to guess what this might mean to him. At best, he was out of pocket the cost of four teams. At the worst, Ralph Burgess would abandon the attempt at working engines on the Pinetop grade. Nothing he could do tonight, nothing he could try and foresee, would in any way change things.

Accepting this stoically, typically, he began watching the road below again. The crowd was thickening as more people from town, attracted by the sound of the cave-in, climbed out the head of Cedar Street and around the southward-swinging bend above to this spot. Once he was sure he saw Sheila walk into the light of the fire burning on the far side of the hole, though an instant later her figure was lost to sight in the jam of people off there.

In another few moments he knew he couldn't be mistaken in recognizing a man's towering shape, and a shorter one alongside the first. Sam Akers and Ralph Burgess stood at the far rim of the crater arguing something, this becoming apparent when the engineer shortly lifted an arm in a quick, angry motion pointing into the south, his arm then making a swinging gesture toward the higher hills.

Bill supposed they must be talking about the tunnel. The suspicion of this was no sooner with him than his doubt about the tunnel having caused this cave-in was weakening. The bore through the mountain might in fact not follow a straight line to Granite, in which case it was entirely possible that it cut under this section of the foothills.

Thinking of the tunnel, it occurred to him that news of the accident must have reached Akers' camp by now, that the place might be all but deserted as curiosity attracted the crew to this spot.

All at once deciding something, he climbed awkwardly to the saddle, reined the claybank on around and then up through the trees. He was going to have a look at the tunnel.

Sam Akers had said, "Wait for me, Sheila," stepping from his horse and running down the road to make his way through the crowd milling around the edge of the gaping crater.

Sheila had watched him join a man she knew but slightly, Ralph Burgess, and afterward she had sat motionless for several minutes letting her emotions quiet, trying not to think of the accident or of that tense moment with Sam Akers just before the awesome thunder of the cave-in had reached them.

Her excitement and alarm were gone when she finally tied the roan and walked on down to join the crowd, careful to keep her distance from Akers. It was as she approached the near edge of the hole that Early Jordan was pulled from the opposite side of it, and a vast thankfulness ran through her when she saw that the old man wasn't hurt, wasn't even badly shaken.

She wanted to talk to him and started across there when he abruptly hurried away and down the road, not seeing her. And as he disappeared she stopped and took her first deliberate look into the hole.

Scarcely noticing the engine and the tilted log runners of the massive sled, her glance was held in pitying, angry fascination by the two dead geldings. And suddenly the barrier she had held against all thought of the accident's meaning was beaten aside. These were Bill Tenn's animals. Their stark stiffness and the harness tangled about them were eloquent of the finality of his lost gamble.

She suddenly felt a deep chill run through her, chill that had nothing to do with the air's biting coldness. And she turned quickly away, no longer able to bear the sight below. Hurrying out from the crowd and then heading back up the road, she was gripped by a helpless anger. And all at once she was longing to be with Bill Tenn, longing to be able to offer him her sympathy and reassurance.

But in another moment she was being honest enough with herself to admit that she longed to be with him for still another reason. Oddly, incomprehensibly, he seemed to be the one person she could think of who might calmly and dispassionately help her unknot the tangle of her own troubles right now. For she was confused and bewildered, for the first time in her life really doubting her judgment.

This torment, the aftermath of Sam Akers' bland denial of having seen Buck on the street the night of the killing, was almost as strong as her worry over Bill and the seriousness of the blow this accident might represent for him. Akers' lie held frightening and unsettling implications. This man she had trusted and liked so much might well be Buck's killer.

The realization of how wrong she had been about Sam Akers shook her deeply. She desperately needed someone to confide in, someone to tell her she had been neither naïve nor weak in liking the big man, someone to help her see the truth about him. And she knew instinctively that she would find this understanding in Bill Tenn.

She was struck now by the incongruity of looking upon a comparative stranger much as she would have regarded an old friend, though this didn't at all lessen her conviction that her instinct was a right one. No single experience had ever worked such a surprising and unlooked for change in her outlook as had that brief interval with Bill yesterday. She could still recall with a measure of awe and wonder the impressions she had brought away with her, the expressiveness and quick response she had found in his lean face and dark eyes, the innate gentleness in him. But the most surprising and likeable thing about the man had been his quiet cheerfulness in the face of odds that would have disheartened and embittered most others. It was still hard to believe that she had only two short days ago despised him when tonight the thought of him roused such a feeling of tenderness, of actual fondness in her.

As she climbed into the deepening shadows toward the tree where she had tied the roan, she was wondering where he might be tonight. It occurred to her that his luck might have run out today, that he might right now be in the Granite jail, or perhaps even dead. She wouldn't let her thought dwell on this grim possibility, though she did soberly admit another thing, that his deep hip wound might be a great deal more serious than either of them had realized yesterday.

Just now the distant chant of a pack of night-hunting coyotes sounded eerily from the valley below town, bringing her an awareness of the mystery and loneliness of this wild tangle of hills. Off to the north the pulsing bright pattern of the stars vaguely outlined the ghostly black pyramid of Baldy peak. Reminded even more strongly of Bill, her worry about him heightened to a pitch that was close to desperation.

She was pulling the roan's reins from a stunted pine when suddenly, unexpectedly, the deep tones of Sam Akers' voice sounded from close below to intrude upon her thoughts. ". . . not even in line with this,

Ralph. Going down there's a waste of time."

"Waste or not, I'm having a look at that drain tunnel."

Turning, Sheila saw Burgess astride a short-coupled pony and Akers walking alongside him some thirty yards down the road. They were coming toward her, and in another moment she heard the big man speak again. "There's only one other thing it might be. That air shaft we started and never finished. We were working rotten rock when we quit the job. But, hell man, this hole's forty feet across and . . ."

He checked his words momentarily. Sheila stood very still, hoping he wouldn't see her, finding the prospect of being with him again tonight exceedingly distasteful. But a moment later she felt a stab of disappointment as he called, "So there you are, Sheila."

She made no reply, his words serving strangely to quiet the confused run of her thoughts so that she could coolly watch his approach as he left Burgess and came toward her.

"Couldn't find you down there." His too-ready smile broke his heavy-featured face as he stopped in front of her. "Ralph and I are having to go down to the tunnel right now. But could I stop by at the house later on?"

It wasn't in Sheila Flynn's makeup to tolerate the doubt and uncertainty that were in her just now. And because she had to know about this man once and for all, had to repair her damaged self respect, she ignored what he had said and told him, "Sam, before this happened we were talking about the night Buck died."

"So we were. What about it?"

The weak glow of the distant fire let her make out the sudden impassivity that settled across his face, and now she bluntly told him, "You were seen on the street that night with Buck. Had you forgotten?"

Akers' massive frame swayed as though under the impact of a hard blow. His shadowed face seemed to tighten in alarm or rage. Then he was saying sharply, "Whoever said that lied."

Sheila shook her head. "The person who said it doesn't know the meaning of a lie."

"By God, I don't take this." Akers suddenly reached out with both hands, gripped her arms and shook her roughly. "Who's been smearing me? Out with it. Who has?"

He was far different from the man she had known, a frightening savagery in him now. For an instant Sheila was really afraid of the depths of violence she glimpsed in him. But then a sudden loathing rose in her, her temper flared and she brought her hands up to throw them sharply outward and break free of his tight grip.

"Sam, be careful. Be very careful of what you say."

"Careful of what *I say?*" He was losing control of himself. "They don't get away with it. I'll break the man in two that said it. Damned if you stand there —"

Sheila struck him hard across the face, the blow laying a flat, sharp sound across the stillness. She had moved before quite knowing what she was doing, his blunt words having roused an uncontrollable fury in her. And now sheer instinct made her step quickly back out of his reach so that his suddenly reaching hands hung suspended in a grotesque gesture of ridiculous helplessness.

"Here, here, you two."

Sheila hadn't been aware of Burgess sitting his horse beyond Akers until this moment. She turned now, swung astride the roan and roughly reined in on Akers so that he had to lunge aside or be run down. She looked at him as she came abreast of him, saying, "I think I know now. I'm sure of it."

"Sure of what?" His tone was suddenly deflated as he saw he had gone too far. "Sheila, you've got to give a man a chance. You've got me dead wrong. Now hold on while . . ."

Sheila was riding on away from him. And

in another moment she heard Burgess break out sharply, "Let her go. And what the hell you mean, roughing her the way you did?"

Bill let the claybank drift down out of the trees and wade the snow behind the nearest tent, his senses keening the night for any sound or movement that would signal danger. The camp seemed deserted, though several of the bigger tents glowed dully with lantern light and two fires off along the grade patterned the blackness with blobs of orange brightness.

One of the fires half silhouetted Akers' log office, sight of the squat building rousing a blend of quiet anger and wonder in Bill. Recollection of Akers' crude attempt to take advantage of him that first morning still rankled, though he found it hard to believe that so much had happened in the few days since then.

The tunnel's broad, high maw lay a scant fifty yards to his left now and he put the horse toward it with the reassuring silence beginning to ease the hard alertness in him. He was coming in on the hole, was perhaps thirty feet from it, when all at once he saw a faint glow thinning the blackness of the opening.

He sharply pulled the claybank to a stand and afterward had perhaps four seconds in which he could have turned and ridden across to the cover of the nearest thicket of oak. He didn't, instead holding his high frame motion-less as a man carrying a lantern trudged from the tunnel's mouth and toward him along the snowy grade.

Suddenly the man saw the horse and halted. He lifted the lantern high, took his full look at Bill, who now reined toward him with his right side hidden, with right hand unbuckling coat so that it hung open. And as Bill stopped the claybank close alongside the grade, the man let the lantern fall to his side again, ask-ing, "You been up there?"

The question puzzled Bill. But then as he read no suspicion or even surprise on the other's face, he finally caught its meaning and nodded, drawling, "It's a mess."

"Anyone found the boss yet?"

"He's up on the road." As an afterthought, wondering quite deliberately if he would be believed, Bill added, "I was supposed to get down here and see how bad it is."

The man frowned now, eyeing Bill more closely. "Don't think I've seen you around." But then he shrugged, saying, "Nothing bad about it just yet. The upper end of that air shaft has fallen in. But it could be bad if the whole thing caved on us. Akers had better get it timbered in so it can't block the drain tunnel."

Unable to make much sense of the words,

Bill nevertheless commented, "It was the main tunnel the boss was worried about."

"Why? This main hole's 'way out of line with the road."

Bill nodded. "So it is." He tilted his head toward the tunnel mouth. "Anyone else in there?"

"Nope. I been on my own." The man waded the deep snow at the grade's edge now, walking in on the claybank and offering the lantern. "Here, you'll want this. Me, I'm going up the road to get in on the fun."

Bill's breath left his chest in a slow, inaudible sigh as he took the lantern and then watched the other walk off into the shadows along the grade. And as he lost sight of the man he debated what to do, ride on into the big hole or leave here. The mention of a drain tunnel and an air shaft carried little meaning for him. Regardless of that, this encounter had given him the answer he had come here to get.

He was lifting the lantern, about to blow it out and ride on away, when abruptly Akers' crewman was calling, "Forgot something. You better swap that light for another. It's close to running dry."

Lifting a hand in acknowledgment, Bill knew he couldn't leave here just yet without running the chance of rousing the man's suspicions. So he put the claybank up onto the grade and rode into the tunnel's mouth.

Lanterns hung on spikes driven into the granite every hundred feet or so to light the expanse of the big hole as far ahead as he could see. Wary at the thought that the man behind might still be watching him, he reined over to the first lantern and exchanged it for the one he was carrying. Then, knowing that his shape must be strongly silhouetted by the line of lanterns ahead, he rode on, feeling the air gradually become warmer, the slap of the claybank's shoes filling the man-made cavern with loud clacking echoes.

He held the horse to a walk, wanting to waste time until he could be fairly sure of turning around and riding out of here without being seen. Just now he was beginning to wonder how much he would be risking by riding into town tonight on the off chance of seeing Sheila or of finding John Updyke in his office, and to wonder bleakly whether or not the accident would mean that Burgess would abandon the hauling of the engines.

All at once he noticed a shoulder-high hole in the right wall close ahead, shortly knowing it must be the drain tunnel on seeing a channeled shallow stream of water at the base of the wall that flowed into it. Coming abreast of it, he reined in, holding out the lantern and bending over to look into the hole. Straightening, he glanced back along the line of lanterns, not knowing how far he had ridden and supposing he might still be within sight of the man out there.

Because of that, and also perhaps because he was curious, he stiffened his sore leg and gingerly swung down out of the saddle limping across the tunnel's wide floor then to loop the reins over a lantern spike on the far wall, his hand settling to the front of his coat and feeling the reassuring bulk of the Colt's at his belt as he walked on back and stooped to enter the tunnel.

He had taken only ten hunched-over strides before he felt the water beginning to leak through his boots. He stopped then, standing against one wall and out of the stream, half decided to wait out several minutes here and then go to the claybank. But now his curiosity to see exactly what had undermined the road was growing stronger. Wondering whether or not he should go on, he considered the risk he would be running.

Akers' man had said that he had been alone in the tunnel. How long it would be before more of the crew returned to inspect the damage was a guess he wasn't prepared to make. But if he was to spend any time waiting here he might as well be using that time.

So he went on, deciding to give himself five minutes before turning back. He felt shut in, oppressed by the narrow confines of this hole, and walked as fast as he could without hurting his sore leg. And in less than two minutes the lantern's reaching glow showed him a plank door standing open close ahead half blocking the width of the hole.

Rounding that door, he looked into the opening of a climbing side shaft with footholds cut into the rock. This was undoubtedly the shaft Akers' crewman had mentioned. He started climbing it and within fifty feet came to the bottom of a ladder angling off to the right.

He went up the ladder one awkward step at a time, pausing when he reached its end and debating whether or not to take still another ladder climbing on even more steeply. At length he went on up it feeling some misgivings but nevertheless giving in to his curiosity.

The end of this second ladder gave onto a broad and irregular ledge at the inner edge of which a third ladder climbed into the shut-in blackness overhead. Rock rubble lay scattered across the uneven platform, a mound of it burying the foot of the ladder. And with the thought, *Must be getting close,* he started for the foot of the ladder.

That instant the soft-booming tones of a voice from far below sounded up out of the shaft. He wheeled sharply around, experiencing a moment of numbing alarm as his glance shuttled around this rock walled pocket. He made out an irregular indentation in the granite some ten feet away in the deep shadows to his left, and as the sound of the voice came once more, this time more loudly, he limped across there, levered open the lantern and quickly blew it out.

He was crouching with his back to the rock, Buck Flynn's Colt's in his hand, when he heard a voice that was unmistakably Ralph Burgess's echo hollowly up out of the shaft from close below. "Why didn't I know about this?"

"You were told about it."

Every muscle in Bill's rangy frame tightened as he recognized Sam Akers' deep voice answering the engineer. Then in another moment Burgess was saying querulously, "I wasn't told that this confounded hole wandered every which way through the mountain. A shaft's supposed to be dug in a straight up line."

"We kept to the soft rock to save work."

Now Bill could hear the scrape of their boots on the ladder directly below as the engineer dryly stated, "Somebody's head was soft not to have known you were right under the road, Sam."

"Listen, Buck was in charge of this, not me."

The engineer made no response. Suddenly Bill saw a lantern's glow palely light the head of the ladder. And in a few more seconds Burgess's head and shoulders rose above the platform's edge.

The engineer climbed from the shaft and stood eyeing the next ladder, running a hand across his damp forehead as Akers' massive shape laid a wider, taller shadow alongside his on the far wall.

"How much further?"

"I'd say no futher at all from the looks of the rubble lying there. It's come down from above."

Burgess stepped across and looked overhead. "What's up there?"

"Only more of same."

"But how much more? How much higher does it go?"

"Search me. I've only been up here once. Forty, fifty feet maybe."

"There must've been a big hole above."

Sam Akers only shrugged, whereupon the smaller man told him, "Let's give it a try," and started up the ladder.

Bill had been breathing shallowly, his wary

glance not straying from Akers. And just now as Akers followed Burgess, Bill heard the big man sniff audibly and saw him look around to stare squarely into the shadows. "What's that I smell?"

The engineer stopped and looked down. "Smell?"

"Like a lantern smoking."

"You're carrying one, aren't you?"

Not at all satisfied, still frowning in puzzlement, Akers reluctantly stepped to the ladder and began the climb. And as Bill sighed gently in relief on seeing the man's legs lift out of sight into the upper shaft, Akers complained, "Someone's been in here ahead of us. There was that jughead down below, and now this oil stench."

"Maybe he's up above."

"Maybe. But who can it be?"

Burgess's reply was lost in its own low echo. And now Bill came quickly erect, jamming the Colt's into belt and stepping toward the head of the ladder leading below, reaching out with a boot to feel for the ledge's edge. Except for the fading faint glow of the lantern overhead he was surrounded by a pressing blackness, suddenly feeling trapped, wanting to be out of here.

The engineer's voice sounded hollowly down to him again now. "Looks like this is as far as we go," the words lifting an urgency in him. His boot all at once kicked an upright of the ladder leading downward. And as he shifted the lantern from one hand to the other, then reached out for a grip on the ladder, Burgess's voice came sharply down out of the shaft. "What the hell is this?"

"Looks like a chunk of rock," came Akers' reply.

"Rock, sure. But look at that color."

"What about it?"

"What about it?" the other echoed. "Lord, man, it's silver. Silver sulphide."

That double mention of the word silver froze Bill Tenn in the act of stepping onto the ladder. Barely a minute ago he had heard Sam Akers mention Buck Flynn's name. And suddenly what the engineer had just said gave sharp meaning to what Sheila had told him of Mary Stone's stubborn insistence that Buck and Akers had mentioned silver in their argument on the street that night before the killing.

"Have it your own way, Ralph. It's silver." The hollow, echoing distortion of Sam Akers' voice failed to rob it of its deadly serious quality. "Only if you want to get your tunnel dug you'll talk no such foolishness to anyone else."

There was a long moment's silence before Burgess plainly said, "It's no foolishness, Sam.

This is a chunk of real high grade."

"Suppose it is?"

"What're you so sore about?" the engineer wanted to know.

"No one's sore. But listen, Ralph. There's hard rock men in this camp. Let one of them hear of this and where does that leave me? I'd —"

The other's low laugh cut across Akers' words. "Now I see what you're getting at. Don't want the word to get around, eh? In that case this is between you and me. But the two of us could do worse than to look into this on our off time, Sam."

"I'm no miner. And right now I've got other things to think about than the color of rock. You ready to go down?"

"Guess I am. But I wish I knew what was up there in . . ."

Bill didn't wait for more, hurrying down the ladder even though his sore hip began aching instantly. When he reached the bottom of the ladder he took one sideward step and struck a match, shaking it out as its brief flare showed him the head of the bottom ladder.

He paused briefly below, hearing no sound from the shaft overhead. And now, knowing he could go no further without light, he lit the lantern once more, then went awkwardly down the uneven footholds cut into the rock along the steep incline at the bottom of the hole.

Once he had rounded the door into the drain tunnel he hurried on even faster, shortly feeling a moistness at his hip and knowing he had pulled the wound open. When he saw the weak light outlining the drain tunnel's low mouth he again levered open the lantern and blew it out.

He was wet to the knees and breathing heavily when he finally hobbled across the main tunnel, went astride the claybank and rode on out toward the camp. And just then it suddenly occurred to him that Akers knew who this horse belonged to, for Akers had seen the claybank up on Baldy yesterday.

John Updyke was hurrying down the steps of the *Buena Vista* when Sheila, coming down the street off the pass road after leaving Akers, saw him and called his name, reining her borrowed roan in from the street's center.

The lawyer stepped down into the snow, ducked under the rail and came up to her saying worriedly, "I would be out of town when it happened. Just got back from a drive down the valley. How bad is it?"

She shook her head. "Bad enough, John."

"Anyone hurt?"

"No. But Early came close to being buried.

They got him out." Over a slight pause, she told him, "Bill's teams are gone. Four of them."

"Lucky there weren't more." With a gusty sigh, he observed, "The damnedest things happen to the wrong people. Who'd ever have suspected there was a cave up there. Anyone have any idea how it could've happened?"

"I didn't ask." . . . Sheila's voice was pitched low in disheartenment . . . "This means Bill's through, doesn't it?"

"Through how?" Belatedly catching her meaning, he shook his head. "Don't see why. According to what I've been hearing, the engine's sticking halfway out of the hole. Shouldn't be hard to winch it out and pull it on down here."

A wave of relief that was akin to happiness ran through Sheila. "Can they really do that? Will they let Early go ahead with the rest of the work?"

Updyke smiled meagerly, thrusting his hands in coat pockets and hunching his collar tighter to his neck against the cold. "You don't know Ralph Burgess, girl. That man never gives up on anything. Bill's in business for as long as he can manage to duck the law and help Early over the rough spots."

His words made her remember something and instantly her near-elation was gone. "Bur-

239

gess was up there. So was Sam. John, I asked Sam about meeting Buck that night. He . . . he lied to me again. And I told him I knew he was lying, that I was sure of what really happened."

She saw his thin frame straighten. "What are you sure of?"

"Sam killed Buck. If he didn't, if he wasn't afraid of being found out, why didn't he own up to their having quarreled?" Sheila's tone was edged with real anger as she went on, "He was beside himself when I told him the two of them had been seen together that night. If it hadn't been for Burgess being there Sam would have . . . He had his hands on me. He was shaking me, trying to get me to tell him who had seen him."

The lawyer's eyes had come wider open in amazement. "Sort of a risky thing to do for a man with matrimonial intentions, wasn't it?"

"That's what led up to it." She could feel her face grow hot with humiliation and embarrassment. "You won't believe this, John. But he had just finished offering to take me away from what he called 'slaving' in a boarding house."

"Slaving?" With more wonder than amusement in his glance, Updyke reached up now to lay a hand on her arm and grip it almost fiercely. "This makes the night not such a bad one after all."

"You've known it, haven't you, John? Known what kind of a man he is."

"Don't pin a man down with a question like that. Let's just say I'm not begging you to change your mind about him."

"Why couldn't I have known it long ago, known him for the kind of man he is?"

"He's had the blinders on a lot of people, Sheila. Buck liked him, so why think you should have had some special way of seeing through him?" Updyke's tone had been gentle, yet now as he went on it wore a rougher edge. "But this about his having killed Buck is strong medicine. You don't have a leg to stand on, nothing but a woman's hunch."

"I didn't come right out and accuse him of it. What I said was . . . was that I was sure of something. Sure of what I didn't say."

"That's better," he said in obvious relief. "Let him worry it around in that sly mind of his. But don't lay yourself open to more trouble by letting yourself be caught alone with him. If he did what we think, there's no telling what —"

"John, you just said 'we.' Then you've suspected him, too?"

"I've suspected everyone but myself and Bill," was the lawyer's noncommittal answer.

"You've never once doubted Bill, have

you?" At his shake of the head, she asked, "Is this enough to take to Red Bushrod? Or to the sheriff?"

"Afraid not. We'll have to hope for more than we have against the man just now."

"But suppose Bill runs into more trouble meantime? He's . . . he's been shot once. It could happen again."

He peered up at her in an oddly speculative way, all at once surprising her by saying, "This thing's gone a bit ahead of me. I hadn't known you felt quite this way about Bill."

The man's strong instinct for knowing what lay in the minds of others wasn't to be argued. He had labelled something Sheila herself had only barely begun to recognize. Suddenly and with no doubt whatsoever she realized now that her regard for Bill Tenn was as foreign to what she had thought to be a genuine fondness for a man as was her feeling toward Sam Akers tonight compared to what it had been a week ago. Akers had never been able to stir the depth of emotion in her that even the thought of Bill could rouse. And just now she unashamedly, even proudly, let John Updyke glimpse what lay in her heart as she looked down at him.

"I hadn't known it either, John. But since that's the way it is, I'd give anything to be able to help him."

"That's a tall order, Sheila. Unless Early could help. I'm on my way up there now to try and find him." With a spare smile, Updyke added, "Wonder how it'll feel if I run into Akers and he begins asking me things. Things like why I sent you up to Bill yesterday."

He touched his hat, said, "I'll be on my way," and was stepping away from the roan when she stopped him by calling, "I'll be at the house, in case you learn anything."

"Chances are I won't. But I'll drop around anyway."

"And John." As his glance swung up to her once more, she told him hesitantly, "If the old man can get word to Bill, have him tell him that I . . . tell him that . . ."

She shook her head in irritation as she ran out of words, answering John Updyke's knowing smile with one of her own, saying softly, "Never mind, it'll keep till I can see Bill myself."

"That's better," the lawyer drawled as he turned out across the street once more.

Bill Tenn walked the claybank around the wide tangle of an oak thicket and then into the head of the alley backing the houses on the east side of Alder Street, his hand pressed to the moistness of his sore hip as he wondered if he was taking a foolish chance in riding on

243

into town. The glow of a fire thinned the night's obscurity in the upper distance toward the hills, and it occurred to him that a superstitious man, with the evidence of tonight's accident marked by the fire up there, would long ago have decided that his luck had deserted him. But he was enough of a fatalist to smile sparely at the thought and at once dismiss it.

His feet and legs had five minutes ago gone briefly numb as he left the tunnel and the sharp cold froze the cloth of his pants and turned his boots stiff. But he was warm now, though he could faintly hear the cuffs of his frozen pants scraping his boots as he looked on ahead into the near blackness.

The starlight let him faintly see that little traffic had been along the alley since the end of the storm, for the heavy drifts were broken by only one set of broad bobsled tracks and the hoof holes of only a few animals. The deep snow let the claybank move without a sound except for the creaking complaint of the cinch straining against the latigo. And now the darkness and the stillness were loosening the strain of the wariness that had held him a minute ago as he made his way from the tunnel through the work camp to swing down toward the town.

But shortly a measure of that hard alertness

was with him again as he came to the first houses and was forced to expose himself by riding through an occasional reach of light shining from a kitchen window. Once his nerves snapped taut as a dog barked viciously from a back porch and then ran out to snap at the claybank's heels. But a few moments later he was in the grip of another emotion, a nostalgia blended with a strong awareness of being an outcast as a lighted dining room's uncurtained window bay let him glimpse a family — a man and woman and three children — sitting around a supper table.

He could see fire glowing in the window of a stove's door across the room, could even make out the man's warm smile as he reached over to rumple the hair of the youngest boy. And the scene brought him a momentary sense of hopelessness and loneliness. But then he forced himself to think of his reasons for being out here alone in the night, to think of Sheila and John Updyke and, lastly, of the indictment the law had put upon him. And as the quiet rebellion against the unfairness of it all rose in him again he was no longer disheartened and unsure of himself.

He came abruptly to the end of this stretch of alley as it met the upper cross street and he pulled the horse to a stand and sat for a full minute studying the neighboring walk and the shadowed distance to a hump-roofed barn marking the alley's entrance across the street's snowy width. Finally he rode on across there at a jog, and had gone fifty yards into the lower alley before he let his breath go in a slow, relieved exhalation.

Now the outbuildings along the alley were closer together and flanking him on both sides. He passed a wood shed, an empty corral, another barn opposite what appeared to be a warehouse. He began peering toward the street and shortly saw the houses give way to a closer rank of buildings, most of them single-storey and false fronted. And then he looked ahead to see light feebly marking the alley's mouth where it joined the main cross street just east of the hotel corner.

He swung out of the alley now, away from the street and across a vacant lot marked by snowed-over mounds of trash and scrubby bunches of oak brush, angling toward the outline of a shed. He found the shed empty, its door sagging, and he led the claybank inside and tied the reins to a split wall board. Wading back through the snow, then crossing the alley to stride into the obscurity of a between buildings passageway, he could feel the bandage pulling at the sore spot along his thigh and knew that the wound was no longer bleeding.

Stopping at the dark head of the passageway

he was relieved at finding the stretch of plank walk to both sides unlighted, heavy with shadow. And as he eased a shoulder against the building to his left, leaving his right hand clear, he pulled the wide hat low on his forehead and then thrust hands in the ragged pockets of the canvas coat, fairly sure that his shape wouldn't be sighted by the casual eye of any passerby.

Obliquely to his right, the strong blaze of lamplight from the hotel lobby and veranda silhouetted a pair of men coming toward him along the walk. And shortly he could hear one of them saying,

". . . had you from the beginning, Mart. Never bet a pair against a man that cool."

"But he runs a sandy now and then. I might've taken the hand."

They were coming abreast the passageway and abruptly the man on the outside appeared to be looking squarely at Bill. But then as his stride didn't break, and as he observed, "Sure. But for every time he'd be running his bluff there'd be three times when he wasn't," the tightening of Bill's tall frame eased a little. And a moment later as they walked steadily away from him it was gone and he felt more secure in this deep shadow.

He had come here for information and now began wondering how to go about getting it.

He would have to speak to someone, preferably to a lone man. But as the minutes passed, and as men and women came along this walk in twos and threes, never singly, he began thinking that he might have gone to all this trouble and risk for nothing.

A light traffic was going in and out of the *Buena Vista*'s saloon doors, and diagonally across the street a steady trickle of supper customers kept the door slamming on a restaurant. A bobsled pulled by a team of bays trotted past, the harness bells filling the street's shallow canyon with a pleasant jangling. A lone rider passed in the opposite direction, followed shortly afterward by a pair.

Bill scarcely noticed the two until suddenly he was hearing Sam Akers' deep voice saying something unintelligible. His glance swung sharply to the riders, seeing that the second man was Burgess. They went on past the intersection and parted there, Burgess turning in at the hotel and Akers continuing on down the street.

Sight of Akers made Bill more determined than ever at carrying out his reason for having come here. And in three more minutes he was seeing his chances strengthen as a lanky, half-grown boy crossed the intersection and started toward him along this near walk.

The youngster had come on perhaps twenty

strides when abruptly he detoured to the walk's edge and began jumping to reach an icicle hanging from the lip of a wooden awning. Finally he knocked it loose and waded out into the snow behind an empty tie rail to retrieve it. He put it in his mouth and began sucking it as he came on, following the edge of the walk now and hooking an arm about each post to swing out and around it.

When he was still twenty feet distant, Bill eased out of the passageway, turned his back to the boy and sauntered obliquely out across the walk. He was standing there, leaning against a hitching post, as the youngster approached. At the last possible moment he looked around, saying, "Son, I'm lost. Can you tell me where to find the Flynn house?"

The boy halted, looking up incuriously at this tall man as he took the icicle from his mouth. "Ed's or Buck's?"

"Buck's."

"He's dead, mister. If you're —"

"I know that. Just wanted to pay his mother a visit."

The boy's frown was plainly visible then as he objected, "You'll catch 'em at supper, Sheila and her mother."

"Then I'll wait a spell. But where's the house?"

Pointing down the street, the youngster answered, "Down there next to Murchison's."

Sighing gently and holding a tight rein on his impatience, Bill asked, "And which house would be Murchison's?"

"The white one. The one with . . . Let's see, the one with the iron fence."

"Then Flynn's is the one beyond?"

"No, the one this side."

Bill nodded. "Much obliged." He turned away then and went back along the walk toward the intersection.

Johnny Grubb continued on up the street as far as the tobacco shop, where he stopped to jam his icicle into the mouth of the grinning wooden Indian standing on the doorstep. Further on, he crossed over to try and tilt the frozen-solid rain barrel under the downspout of Meador's *Mercantile*. Then, hearing the bells of a bobsled sounding from upstreet, he walked on out and waited, presently hitching a ride on the sled by hopping the nearest back runner.

He had almost reached the intersection below when suddenly, in near terror, he remembered where he had several days ago seen the stranger who had stopped him to ask the way to Flynn's. He started shouting, "It's him! Right here in town. Tenn! I tell you I saw him."

The driver of the sled glanced around in

some surprise. But then Johnny shouted at him, "Tenn! I just saw him!" and the man hauled his team to a stand, asking sharply, "How's that? Tenn, you say?"

In two more minutes a crowd was gathering at the street's center, ringing the sled.

VII

Bill Tenn had left the street to go back to the claybank and ride a wide circle on out around the end of the cross street before angling in on the lower reach of Alder, thus being left completely unaware of the crowd milling around the bobsled and young Johnny Grubb above the intersection at the center of town. He reached Alder Street by coming in across the deep drifts of a vacant lot, and by sheer accident found himself squarely facing a white house.

Riding warily toward it, he shortly made out an ornate fence enclosing its yard, his glance afterward swinging eagerly to the house above. But what he saw brought him a sharp disappointment, for the strong lamplight shining from the two front windows and the upper glass half of the door lit the porch so brightly that he at once abandoned any notion of going onto the porch.

Because he gave the house such a brief inspection, immediately peering into the downstreet darkness in wondering how he could reach the back lots, he failed to notice

Sam Akers' horse standing at the hitching post beyond a low-growing cedar tree at the Flynn gate.

Had he seen the animal the next half hour would have had an entirely different outcome. As it was, his impatience made him rein the claybank down the street and in along the line of a packed wagon track paralleling the iron fence on the lower side of the Murchison house. He came to a shed, rounded it into the alley and turned back past the rear of the lot.

Light shining from one rear window of the Flynn house across the adjoining yard's friendly blackness stirred a small excitement in him at the realization that he might be seeing Sheila in another minute or two. For a moment he was experiencing that same sense of awe and humility that had gripped him so strongly yesterday when he had been with her. And as he came down out of the saddle alongside an open-fronted wood shed, tied the reins and walked in on the house's rear stoop, he was soberly admitting that his hunger for another glimpse of her was what had brought him here instead of taking him to John Updyke with the word of what he had overheard in the tunnel shaft.

The past few days had bred a heightened caution in him, so that now as he reached the steps he climbed them soundlessly, turning his tall frame sideways and out of a weak shaft of lamplight shining through a small window alongside the door. He eased into line with the window, peered through it and saw Sheila's mother standing not three feet away.

Brigid Flynn was doing the supper dishes. And as Bill watched her, thinking back on what Sheila had said yesterday of the woman's uncertain animosity toward him, he experienced a let down as sharp as any he could remember. In his eagerness to see Sheila again he had blithely overlooked this possibility of encountering her mother instead.

He stood watching her for all of a minute, studying her serene face in trying to decide whether or not to risk trusting her. A week ago Brigid Flynn had thought him her son's killer. Regardless of what Sheila had said yesterday, he had no way of knowing whether or not she still regarded him as being guilty of that brutal murder. He tried to think of something he could say to her, of some way of persuading her to listen while he explained his reason for being here.

Finally it was nothing but an instinctive belief in her goodness and sense of fairness that decided him. Without at all knowing what he was to say, he moved away from the window and knocked on the door, afterward removing his hat.

He had hoped to get inside the house before she could recognize him. Yet that hope instantly died when the door opened on a full glare of light. Brigid Flynn stood there holding a lamp and staring squarely at him.

There was a moment when the wide-eyed, shocked look loosening her face almost panicked him, made his rangy frame tighten at the certainty that she was about to scream. But then she was breathing softly in alarm, "Come in. Hurry before someone sees you," to leave him weak with relief.

Bill stepped into the kitchen and pushed the door shut as she backed away from him. Leaning against the door, he said quietly, "I hadn't thought it would be quite this way. You have my thanks, Mrs. Flynn."

She was suddenly putting a finger to her lips and staring toward an open door leading to the front of the house. Without further explanation she crossed the room, softly closed the door and turned to reach up and replace the lamp in its bracket on the wall.

Facing him once more, a slow, unaccountably tender smile lit her face. "So you're safe, William Tenn. Sheila will want to know." An odd, probing quality came to her glance then. "I must get to know you. Something happened to Sheila yesterday, something good."

The awe that gripped Bill just now was even greater than that of a moment ago at the unexpectedness of this welcome. And as he groped for something to say she told him, "She'll want to see you. But we must be careful. Sam Akers stopped by not ten minutes ago. Sheila's with him in the front room now."

"Then I'd better wait outside."

"No." Brigid Flynn's glance went to a second door along the kitchen's inside wall. She motioned him to follow and crossed the room to open that door. "You'll wait down there in the cold cellar. Just in —"

The sudden booming echo of someone pounding heavily on the front door sounded back to them, cutting across her words. She gave Bill a look of alarm and wordlessly reached out to push him toward a flight of steps beyond the door leading downward.

Sheila hurried out of the parlor frowning in annoyance at the heavy knocking once more rattling the front door's frosted glass. Irritated as she was by the insistent pounding, she was nonetheless thankful for the unlooked-for interruption. For these past few minutes with Sam Akers had held a strong undercurrent of tension, even animosity, as he pried at her stubborn refusal to discuss what she had heard of his having been seen with Buck on the street

the night of the killing.

She opened the door now, recoiling a [?] at sight of Red Bushrod standing on the po with a gun levelled at her. He quickly let weapon fall and, dropping it in holst reached up to touch his hat. "Sorry, Shei but I couldn't make out who it was."

"Who were you expecting it to be?"

"Tenn maybe." His probing glance wei narrow-lidded as he took in the way her slen der body straightened in surprise. "He wa seen on the street a few minutes ago. Talkec to Wayne Grubb's youngster. Asked how to find his way here."

"But I . . ."

Sheila was as confused as she was alarmed, hardly knowing what to think of what the marshal was saying. And as her words trailed off, Bushrod looked beyond her to say, " 'Evening, Sam."

She turned, unaware until now of Akers having followed her. The big man was scowling and his voice wore a rough edge as he asked, "What's this? Tenn around here?"

"Looks like he headed this way anyway." The marshal came in and closed the door, eyeing Sheila in an apologetic way. "After the other night I'm afraid I can't just take your word on this, Sheila." He abruptly glanced on back across the hallway, nodding and say-

ing uneasily, "Sorry to make such a fuss, Mrs. Flynn. We're looking for Tenn."

Sheila turned to find her mother standing at the entrance to the back hallway just as the older woman asked, "But why here? You certainly can't think —"

"He asked his way to this house, ma'am."

Brigid Flynn gave the law man a stare of convincing puzzlement before looking at Sheila. "You and Sam would have known if anyone had come in the front door. And I've been in the kitchen the last half hour."

Red Bushrod stood a moment in awkward uncertainty before saying, "So long as I have your word, I reckon there's no —"

The sound of heavy, hurried steps crossing the porch made him swing around and open the door. Someone out there excitedly told him, "His horse is out back, Red. Tracked him as far as the path leading from the porch back there to the wood shed. He never left the path, so he's got to be in the house."

Bushrod's accusing glance whipped around to Sheila and her mother. Reaching out to close the door again, he told the man outside, "You keep watch out front and get Jim out back. Shoot if you spot him."

The slam of the door punctuated the finality of his words as he faced Sheila and her mother once more. And it was Sam Akers who spoke

for him by gruffly saying, "Then he is here."

"He is."

Those quiet words, spoken so unexpectedly from beyond Brigid Flynn, made Sheila stiffen and gasp, "Bill!" made Sam Akers jerk around as Bushrod moved quickly out of line with Sheila.

The marshal's hand was lifting to holster as he moved. But when he saw Bill Tenn standing at the head of the dark hallway leading to the kitchen, saw the gun Bill held at his side, he very carefully straightened his arm, empty-handed.

Sheila's face wore a frightened, shocked expression as her mother looked around in alarm at Bill to say, "You should have stayed where I —"

His slow shake of the head cut her short. "No. A man can run and hide only so long. I've finished with both."

There was a quality in his tone, in his way of coolly staring at Akers as though he and the big man were alone in this room, that now had its effect. For the belligerent quality thinned and died in Akers' eyes as he abruptly glanced around at Bushrod to snap, "Do something, Red."

"Not me." The marshal shook his head. "Only you can't get away with this, Tenn. I've got a man out front, another out back."

"So I just heard you say." Bill's glance still clung to Akers as he drawled, "We've a little something to settle here. Red, ask him where he was when Buck was killed. Or maybe you shouldn't. Because he'll only tell you he wasn't anywhere around."

Akers' look betrayed an instant wariness. He even gave himself away by letting his glance stray uneasily in Sheila's direction before he caught himself and burst out, "First Sheila, now you. Who's thought up this lie about my being seen with Buck on the street?"

"Ask him something else, Red." It was as though Bill hadn't heard that angry protest. "Ask him what he and Buck were scrapping about that night."

"Me scrapping with Buck? That's another damned lie. Why would I when he was the best friend I ever had?"

Despite the big man's outraged rejoinder, and in spite of the way he stood glaring as though about to lunge at him, Bill sensed that Akers was very aware of the puzzled scrutiny Bushrod had fastened on him. And because he saw the beginning of a doubt working at the law man, he repeated, "Ask him, Red."

Bushrod scowled. "Well, Sam. What's the answer?"

The marshal's tone was clipped, cold. It had its visible effect on Akers, who swung his head sharply to study first Bushrod, then Sheila. What he saw on their faces made him ask incredulously, in an injured way, "My God, you two believe what this killer's trying to say?"

"I do."

It was Sheila who answered him. His expression instantly showed hurt and bewilderment. "Why? What've I done to have this thrown at me when not a word of it is true? There can't be an answer to an out and out lie. I don't know what he's talking about! Neither does he."

"Ask him something else, Red." Bill's eyes mirrored a faint trace of amusement now. "Ask him about a chunk of rock Ralph Burgess showed him tonight. Ask him if that rock wasn't the reason he killed Buck. Then you can ask him about the drawing of a claim location that was found in Buck's pocket after he died. Ask him —"

Sam Akers suddenly reached out, snatched Sheila's arm and roughly pulled her toward him so that she came between him and Bill's lifting Colt's. Sheila cried out in pain as the big man all at once shoved her hard forward and into Bill, then wheeled sharply in through the parlor doorway.

Bill instinctively reached out and caught Sheila to keep her from falling as the door crashed shut with a violence that rattled the brass fender on the hall tree across the room. He was lunging around her toward the parlor door when he collided with Red Bushrod.

The marshal was jarred off balance and fell to his knees calling, "Get him, Tenn."

Hard on the heel of his words came a loud crash from the parlor followed by a jangle of falling glass. Bill pushed the door open in time to see Sam Akers' massive shape dropping from sight beyond the room's smashed front window and a broken chair that lay below the sill.

He was running toward that window when an unintelligible shout came from the front yard to stop him. After an instant's indecision, he rammed the Colt's in his belt and swung over to the parlor's side window. He raised the blind and threw up the lower sash. He had thrust his upper body through the opening and was lifting a leg over the sill when a gun's hard explosion blasted out of the front yard's obscurity at him.

The bullet smashed the window directly over his head, showering him with shards of broken glass as he threw himself outward and down. He lit on hands and knees in the deep snow, then lunged for the darkness beyond the reach of the window's light.

"Don't shoot Tenn! Stop Akers!"

Bushrod's bellowed words from the

smashed front window rang out across the night an instant before a sudden pound of hooves echoed in off the street. Looking up there Bill had a fleeting glimpse of a high shape astride a horse running away in the darkness. Sam Akers had somehow managed to trick Bushrod's man guarding the front of the house, to get to his horse and away.

And now Bill saw the marshal's man walking in from the walk fence, heard him call, "What the hell's going on here, Red?"

"Why would you let him get away? Go after him."

"How? On foot?"

This angry interchange prodded Bill out of a moment's helpless hesitation, made him wheel and run back along the side of the house half a dozen strides only to halt sharply and swing in with shoulders to the wall as Bushrod's second man suddenly rounded the house's rear corner at a run. The man came on past him without so much as a glance in his direction. He waited two more seconds before going on, before turning the house's back corner and running into the wood shed path.

The claybank was where he had left him, and he jerked the reins free and went to the saddle with the animal already wheeling away into the alley. He at first thought to head for the street and follow Akers, having gathered that neither Bushrod nor his men had ridden here and was consequently afoot and for the moment helpless. But now, realizing how easily Akers could lose himself in this town or beyond its outskirts if he discovered he was being followed, he went on along the alley at a fast jog, groping for a way of heading the big man off.

That's Bushrod's worry, so let him handle it. The thought was no sooner with him than he was coldly thrusting it aside. In that moment he was thinking back over the days since he had ridden down off Dead Man with Early Jordan to Pinetop. Sam Akers had made trouble for him in the beginning and had compounded that trouble many times over. In his scheming, cunning way Sam Akers had taken one man's life and tried to take another's, Bill's. And now Bill knew that this wasn't Bushrod's affair. It was his own.

Suddenly and for the first time in all his experience, Bill Tenn grimly realized what it felt like to hate a man badly enough to kill. The emotion that hit him now bore no relation whatsoever to ordinary dislike or contempt. It was fed by the sharp recollection of the way Akers had so roughly handled Sheila barely a minute ago, by the recurring rancour over Akers having tried to rob him in the beginning, and finally by the heartless, calculating reasons for the man having killed Buck Flynn.

The strong loathing and contempt for Sam Akers welled up out of the core of his being with a deep and scalding intensity that now made him rake the claybank's flanks with the spur, sending the animal on at a hard run. For it all at once struck him how he might just possibly have one last chance of settling his score with Akers before the man could leave the country.

Akers was panicked. He would be taking the quickest way out of here. Knowing that Bushrod and others would soon be on his trail, he wouldn't risk stopping at the hotel or his office. He could ride east into a vast reach of barely settled country, taking his chances on being able to buy food and cross a hundred odd miles of badlands to ride clear of the law. If he headed south he was in trouble, for rugged, torn hill country lay off there, giving way finally to trackless desert. If he swung north he would be in ranch country where he tripled his chances of being seen and recognized.

Sam Akers' best chance lay in riding over Dead Man to Granite, hopping a freight and putting distance between himself and the law.

Coming to the intersection of the main cross street, Bill swung the claybank out along it at a lope. For he was remembering how this street at its end lay close below the last southward swing of the pass road, almost directly below the fire that now glowed above to mark the spot where the Mogul lay in the caved-in glory hole.

The booming thunder of Akers' shot rolling up out of town had made Mary Stone and John Updyke glance away into the downward darkness from where they had been standing alongside the hole in the road looking down upon the buried engine and Bill Tenn's dead mares and geldings.

"Now who could pick this night to be celebrating?" Updyke asked dryly, inwardly hoping that such was the reason for the shot.

Mary Stone shrugged, turning to look back down into the hole, after a long moment asking, "You're sure Burgess won't just give up, John? It would be awful for Bill if he did, wouldn't it?"

"It would be and Ralph won't."

The lawyer was trying to convince himself as well as Mary. Fifteen minutes ago he had been on the point of leaving here and riding back down into town, discouraged by what he had seen and almost convinced that hoisting the Mogul from its near-grave was such a monumental task that even Burgess wouldn't tackle it. But then Mary had walked up the road and into the light of the fire and he had stayed on, wanting to be with her, wanting to talk to her. Now, after more soberly considering what he was seeing, he was beyond being able even to hazard a guess on what Burgess's decision might be.

"John, I was thinking of something this morning. Something that might help Bill."

"If you've thought of something that'll help him you're several steps ahead of me."

She had his strong attention once again. And the way he looked at her, his eyes mirroring a strong unveiled admiration, stirred an unsettling emotion that both pleased her and at the same time made her uneasy. "I was thinking that he should give himself up," she hurried to say. "That he ought to let them put him back in jail until you can find out more about what happened between Buck and Akers that night."

He shook his head. "Not a chance. Bill isn't the kind that gives up." He was all at once looking beyond her. "Here's Early Jordan back again after all. Let's see what he has to say."

She turned and he took her arm to help her across some deep ruts at the road's edge. Very aware of his touch, she gave way to a sudden impulse and tightened her elbow against the pressure of his hand, looking up at him and smiling. "It will come out all right for Bill, won't it?"

"Here's hoping. We may know more in about two more minutes."

They were both feeling a quality of mystery and strangeness, of excitement in this night that had once again brought them together. Neither of them was more than remotely aware of the thinning crowd as they made their way up the road around the edge of the hole toward Early, who was swinging down from the back of an animal he had borrowed in town. John Updyke was right now beginning to look out across his future in a different way, in a way that wasn't at all related to the solitary view he had taken of it a week ago. And as they walked on up to Early the lawyer was pondering the academic question of which was right and proper, mentioning what he had on his mind to Fred Stone first of all or speaking directly to Mary before talking with her father.

They were some twenty feet short of Early when he saw them and trudged over to meet them. His face was set in soberness as he looked at Updyke to announce, "Just come from seeing Burgess. He's giving us a chance."

"How's that, Early?"

"I found me a big winch and plenty of cable down in town. So we start work at sunup trying to lift this confounded thing out of the hole. I'll rig some big logs in sort of a tepee, use block and tackle and pray my rig stays together."

"Think it can be done, Early?"

"I got to think so. If it can't, then Bill loses his shirt. If it can, Burgess lets us go ahead with the other hauls. He calls this a simple act of God."

John Updyke's tone was very solemn as he stated, "Then we'll see that it gets done."

When Sam Akers ran his horse past the first bend in the pass road above the head of Cedar Street and could distinguish figures moving around the crater against the fire's bright glow, he reined hard aside and up through the pines, starting a circle that would carry him unseen around the crowd.

His big frame had been wire tight with apprehension and even over this short distance he had severely punished his horse. Now, thinking back on the fact of his having seen no animals but his own there in front of the Flynn house, some of the panic and the fear left him and he stopped using the spur.

It was beginning to look as though he had made a clean getaway. If he could save the horse and at the same time make a fairly fast ride to Granite he was certain he would be safe. He could ride south to a way station along the railroad. He would be aboard a train, either passenger or freight, before morning.

He took the time now to look back on that final minute at Sheila's house, what had happened having come with such stunning abruptness that he was hardly yet able to grasp the awesome finality of it. His nerve had broken for a reason that was still hard to understand.

Remembering each detail of Tenn's barbed words, he supposed it was the man's remark about Buck's intention of filing a claim that had so suddenly and overwhelmingly told him he could never carry through his bluff of simply denying everything. For that moment it had struck him that if Tenn knew this much he must also know much more.

It had been relatively simple to see how the man might have overheard Burgess's mention of silver tonight, for he had recognized the claybank there in the tunnel and had been bitterly disappointed over not having trapped Tenn in the shaft. He supposed now that he and Burgess had somehow passed him on their climb toward the glory hole. But how Tenn had learned of the other things — of his fight with Buck there on the street, of the silver and of Buck's wanting to file a claim — utterly confounded him. For he had had the evidence of his own eyes as proof that Tenn had come out of the hotel to meet Buck directly after he and Buck had parted.

Oddly enough, it didn't occur to Sam Akers that someone else might have been a witness to his run-in with Buck Flynn. All he knew was that Tenn was the one who had turned Sheila against him, the one who was losing him everything he had to his name.

The cutting chill of the night air and his feeling of urgency to put distance between him and Pinetop brought on a return of a sense of insecurity he had never expected to experience again. He had less than twenty dollars in his pockets. The thousands he was leaving in the bank were as good as gone, for he could never claim them. He was right now little better off than he had been fifteen years ago. He was once more an outcast, a stray living purely by his wits. But for Bill Tenn, none of this would have happened.

There abruptly flashed across his mind's eye one of the many dreams he had had of the day when Sheila would have been his bride. His ire rose instantly, bitterly over the impossibility of ever realizing that dream now. And in thinking of Sheila he was bleakly aware that some unexplained accident of circumstances had drawn her close to Tenn without his even knowing of it. What he had seen yesterday in the hills and what had happened tonight with Sheila below there along the road both told him that the girl had become infatuated with this man who was but a slight cut above a saddle tramp.

This thought more than anything else roused Sam Akers' rancour now until he longed for a way of revenge, for the chance of a final reckoning with Tenn before leaving the country. He knew that such an encounter was an impossibility, yet he had several seconds of downright delight at imagining what he would do to the man if he could but get his hands on him or be able to look at him across the sights of his Smith and Wesson once more as he had right after leaving the Flynn yard barely ten minutes ago.

His rage turned him reckless now, made him rein on down through the trees on a line that would put him barely fifty yards above the crater once he reached the road. Having just thought of his gun, he reached under his coat and drew it now, letting it hang free at his side.

Reaching the road, he found himself well within the fire's light; and he didn't care. He brazenly studied the thinning crowd, recognizing several figures, among them John Updyke, Early Jordan and Mary Stone. It fed his vanity, his sense of power to be this close to people who would shoot him on sight if they only knew what had just happened in town. And as he noticed that no one was apparently looking this way or had seen him, he hefted the Smith and Wesson, momentarily relaxing his tight grip on its handle, smiling thinly, derisively.

He had barely turned up the road and touched his horse's flanks with spurs when suddenly the sound of an animal crashing through a tangle of brush came from close ahead. His glance whipped up there and he saw a rider move onto the road from a thicket of oak barely twenty yards in front of him.

First of all he recognized the claybank as being the same animal he'd seen earlier tonight in the tunnel. An instant later he knew that the tall shape in the saddle must be Tenn's.

A hard elation rose in Akers as he brought up his weapon. He called hoarsely, "Tenn!" as the Smith and Wesson's sights came before his eyes.

Bill Tenn had punished his animal in making this hard, fast climb from the end of the street. On coming into the road he had first glanced toward the fire and the scattered group of people below. A split-second before his name was called he had noticed the rider coming toward him.

The voice could belong to but one man. Instantly, knowing that Akers had the advantage here, seeing the big man's arm lift so suddenly, Bill rowelled the claybank viciously and threw himself outward from the saddle. Powder flame stabbed from the muzzle of Akers' gun as Bill was sweeping his coat aside, reaching for Buck's gun at his belt.

He felt a smashing, numbing blow on his right thigh, felt the claybank tremble. He knew the horse was going down, and he kicked boots free of stirrups as he jerked the Colt's free. Throwing himself outward and clear of the crippled animal, he was facing Akers.

His right leg buckled under him. Yet as he was falling he managed to line the Colt's on Akers' wide chest and squeeze trigger. He saw the man's high shape jolted back by the bullet's impact. Then his shoulder slammed hard against the road's rutted snow and he threw his long frame into a convulsive roll.

There was one lucid, slow-paced moment as he prolonged his roll in which he was struck by the oddity of not having been aware of the blast of either Akers' or his own weapon. A second later he was lying flat to the snow, staring down the road again, to see Akers' animal bolting away, its saddle empty. And then he made out the big man's sprawled bulk lying in the snow barely forty feet away.

He lay there looking across the sights of the

.45 for all of five seconds, his finger lightly pressing the trigger as he waited for Akers to move. He knew remotely that several figures were running up the road between him and the fire. Then two shapes, one much taller than the other, moved into his line of vision. He recognized Early Jordan first as the old man hurried over to him. He didn't know who John Updyke was until the lawyer knelt beside Akers' body.

"Bill, Bill! You hurt?"

Early reached down and took a hold on Bill's arm as Bill swung his legs awkwardly around and tried to stand. And when his right leg gave way the old man cautioned him in an alarmed tone, "Just sit, son. Let me have a look at it. Where did he get you?"

Bill eased back into the snow, putting his hand to his leg and feeling its moistness. Then he thought of something and looked quickly around to see the claybank lying on its side, chest heaving. He nodded toward it, handing Early the Colt's. "Do it right, Early."

Jordan took the gun and walked away. Bill turned his head a moment before the gun's pounding blast smote the stillness. Then he was looking up to see John Updyke standing alongside, to hear the lawyer say, "No bullet ever went straighter than the one you used on Akers."

★ ★ ★

There had been several minutes of utter confusion during which John Updyke and Early Jordan had had to use the persuasion of a pair of Colt's to keep the crowd back from Bill. No amount of explaining would convince the onlookers that they hadn't caught a killer.

But then Red Bushrod, attracted from below by the sound of the guns, had run his horse up the road and taken charge. He brought Bill down to the jail wearing handcuffs and riding a borrowed horse, not listening to Updyke's protest that they should stop at Doc Serles' house on the way. "Won't be the first time the doc's had to climb the stairs to the lock-up to wait on a patient," was his laconic comment, though he had added, "We'll just get a few things sorted out before Tenn goes anywhere else to bed and board."

That had been twenty minutes ago. Serles had climbed the stairs and gone back home after cleaning and bandaging the hole through the thick muscle of Bill's right thigh. Updyke had meantime gone down the street and come back with Sheila. There had been much talking, for Red Bushrod was a hard man to convince.

Now, as Bill finished saying something, the

276

marshal wanted to know, "But where's your proof? I got nothing but your word to go on, nothing —"

"You've got my word and Mary Stone's to go on, Red," John Updyke put in. "I can have Mary here in less than five minutes if you want it straight from her."

Bushrod sighed heavily. "No need, I guess. But . . ."

"But what?"

It was Sheila who put the question. And she went on to underscore her words by insisting, "You saw Sam there at the house, saw his nerve break, saw him run. Isn't that proof enough?"

The marshal reached up and ran a hand through his rust-colored hair, his expression one of bafflement and indecision. "Sure I saw all that. And maybe I take what you're all saying as gospel. But Tenn here's been convicted of murder. I got to mind the law."

"Then we'll go get Judge Haldeman, gather a jury off the street and hold a new hearing on Bill's case tonight," Updyke dryly said.

"The devil with Haldeman," Bushrod bridled. "If I find I've jailed an innocent man I don't need the old coot to tell me it's right to let him go."

Updyke lifted his hands in a palms-up gesture. "Then what are you waiting on, Red?"

Bushrod was all at once convinced. To show it he turned now, reached through the bars of the jail's inner door and unlocked the padlock he had been so careful to fasten on coming in here. He threw the door wide, nodding to Bill, smiling broadly now. "Out you go."

Sheila glanced down at Bill sitting on the bunk, her eyes radiant with a look of sheer delight. And in that moment when the two of them were oblivious of everything but each other, Early Jordan, who hadn't spoken once during all this long interval, reached out and silently took John Updyke's arm, steering him toward the door.

Once they were in the office, the lawyer softly closed the jail door behind Bushrod, saying, "Know what I think, Red? That Burgess is going to want Fred Stone to take over the digging of that tunnel now that Akers is gone."

"Stone? He's not big enough to handle the job."

"He's bigger than Akers ever was in more ways than one, my friend." Updyke went to the stairway door now, looking back at Early. "Come along, Early. I'm seeing Burgess at the hotel. Then you and I are going to make a stop at the bar."

"Sounds good." Early glanced worriedly back at the jail door. "Think Bill can manage on his own?"

"We'll stop by in half an hour or so and see." Updyke opened the door, turned up the collar of his overcoat and led the way out onto the stairway landing. And after he had closed the door he turned to Early and gravely stated, "The right things have happened to the right people tonight, old timer."

Bill and Sheila heard the slam of the stairway door. He smiled up at her and, catching his breath, pushed himself erect.

"You could stay here if it hurts too much to walk, Bill."

"Think I will. Just to see how good it'll feel knowing I can walk out that door any time I get the notion."

He thought of something that laid a look of soberness across his lean face. "Sheila, you're going across to the courthouse in Granite in the morning with John Updyke. And with the drawing Buck made of that claim location."

She nodded, eyeing him with a tenderness he had no way of understanding until she gently told him, "You're trying to do even more than you have already. And to think . . ."

When she hesitated, he asked, "To think what?"

"Of our other time here. Of how different it is now. I . . . Can you ever forgive me for what I came here to do?"

"I'd already forgotten."

"Then it's good to be here with you again, Bill. Good because now we can forget that other time and always remember this one."

It took him a long moment to grasp what she had said, to convince himself that she had meant it exactly as it had sounded. Then he was reaching out to gather her in his arms. And as she tilted her head and her lips met his he knew that the bad days had ended, that only good ones lay ahead.

Peter Dawson is the *nom de plume* used by Jonathan Hurff Glidden for all of his fiction. It was also used once by Frederick Faust, better known as Max Brand, for a magazine story, and by Otis Gaylord for a series of eight novels. The name itself is derived from a popular brand of Scotch whiskey. Glidden was born in Kewanee, Illinois, and was graduated from the University of Illinois with a degree in English literature. He came first to write Western fiction because of prompting from his brother Frederick Dilley Glidden who wrote Western fiction under the pseudonym Luke Short. In his career as a Western writer, he has written sixteen Western novels and over 120 Western novelettes and short stories for the magazine market. Glidden from the beginning was a dedicated craftsman who revised and polished his fiction until it shone as a fine gem. His Peter Dawson novels are noted for their adept plotting, interesting and well developed characters, their authentically researched historical backgrounds, and his stylistic flair. His first novel THE CRIMSON HORSESHOE won the Dodd, Mead Prize as the best Western of the year 1941 and ran serially in Street and

Smith's WESTERN STORY MAGAZINE prior to book publication. During the Second World War, Glidden served with the U.S. Strategic and Tactical Air Force in the United Kingdom. Later in 1950 he served for a time as Assistant to Chief of Station in Germany. After the war, his novels were frequently serialized in THE SATURDAY EVENING POST. In paperback, his books have already sold 25,000,000 copies worldwide and have been translated into numerous foreign languages. Dawson titles such as HIGH COUNTRY, GUNSMOKE GRAZE, and ROYAL GORGE are generally conceded to be among his masterpieces although he was an extremely consistent writer and virtually all his fiction has retained its classic stature among readers of all generations. His short story "Long Gone" (1950) was adapted for the screen as FACE OF A FUGITIVE (Columbia, 1959) starring Fred MacMurray and James Coburn. His earlier classic Western novels are being reprinted in hardcover by Chivers, Ltd., for the English-reading world and many of his longer novel-length titles, beginning with RATTLESNAKE MESA, are appearing for the first time in book form.

The employees of THORNDIKE PRESS hope you have enjoyed this Large Print book. All our Large Print books are designed for easy reading — and they're made to last.

Other Thorndike Large Print books are available at your library, through selected bookstores, or directly from us. Suggestions for books you would like to see in Large Print are always welcome.

For more information about current and upcoming titles, please call or mail your name and address to:

THORNDIKE PRESS
PO Box 159
Thorndike, Maine 04986
800/223-6121
207/948-2962